# OPEN HOUSE

# Open House

### ROBERT COOVER

Evergreen Review Books

Published by Evergreen Review Books, an imprint of OR Books

Visit our website: www.evergreenreview.com

First printing 2023

Library of Congress Cataloging-in-Publication Data:
A catalog record for this book is available from the Library of Congress.

British Library Cataloging in Publication Data:
A catalog record for this book is available from the British Library.

Typeset by Lapiz Digital.

paperback ISBN 978-1-68219-389-1 • ebook ISBN 978-1-68219-390-7

. . . from quarters unseen, comes
a murmur as of bees in the comb . . .

      —*The Confidence Man* (1857), Herman Melville

"I don' think I leave this place so big open wit' so many kaboodle around," says Cookie, pointing at the oil paintings on the walls, the crystal chandeliers, the heavy silverware. Cookie said it was his understanding there would be no locks on the doors, and there weren't. The street door was open, no concierge, a sign at the elevator, pointing everybody up here to the penthouse, which was wide open. "Rich guys don't care," the woman says.

"Maybe it's all fake," I say, though I'm thinking about lifting a few choice items. That saucy little jade statuette, for example, with the knuckled ass and pointy tits. She must be worth a bundle. Cookie, as the woman calls him—her pimp maybe—has been hired to cater a party, and the three of us are up here early to set it up. The cook on his crutches prepares the eats, the woman moves them to chafers and will pass the bite-sized around on silver platters, I mix and serve the drinks. Big crowd expected, so no sit-down service. Too bad. Sit-downs follow rules, stick to timetables, keep drunks in their places. When they can go where they want, they all end up jostling each other at my station. Things break. Spill. Tempers can flare. Mine, for example.

I must have driven past this towering pile hundreds of times without noticing it. Over a hundred floors of swank condos with this penthouse sugar-frosting the top. Don't know why I decided to swing by tonight, but lucky I did. Though I never worked this space before, everything is where I somehow knew it'd be—the professional-grade equipment, the silent exhaust fans, the cooler and ice machine under the bar—everything where it ought to be, and spotless, gleaming like brand new. The other two had brought along a vanload of folding chairs and serving tables, boxes of plastic cups and paper napkins, and we humped it all up on the service elevator, but there were heavy mahogany tables already in place, laid with thick white linens, porcelain, crystal and silver, so we've had to stow all their shit in a back room. It was Cookie who first got wind of the job, but he's a dumb foreigner and clearly doesn't know what the fuck is going on. No need to go back for their cheap food and booze either. The industrial fridge is loaded, the wine racks, nothing but the best. Good thing, too. If I had to go down to the street again, I probably wouldn't have the nerve to come back up. Heights freak me out. It's the one thing wrong with this pad. As soon as she got here, the fat serving woman walked out onto the roof terrace and leaned over. Shouted that she couldn't make out a damn thing. "Come out here and see!" Was she kidding? I raised the first-growth wine magnum I was uncorking and shook my head, staying cool, but, Christ, I nearly shat my pants!

Cookie has found a starched white toque on a counter in the food preparation area, and crowned himself with it. Goes great with his grimy sweat-stained undershirt. He and the woman set out a row of silver chafing dishes on the dining table and light the burners under each, while I, in my new leather apron, uncap the hard stuff in the family bar area and mix some cocktails in the iced pitchers waiting for me in the big fridge. Memory's mostly fucked, but I do remember all the cocktail recipes. Backs are turned and the owners aren't here yet, so I treat myself to a swallow of aged sourmash. Straight from the bottle. And then another. So smooth. Had a few tokes on the street, and they loosened me up, but this works faster and is easier on the throat. Liquid velvet. Keeps me sane, gets my mind off how high up I am. So, OK, a third. My lucky number. Or maybe four is. Yeah, definitely is now.

Grandma had a thing for lucky numbers. Three was one of them, four another, but she had a different one every day. I got dumped on her when my parents went on the road, and her lucky number that day was nine, which was how old I was, proof for her I'd bring her luck. Silly old twat, but she was good to me and I dug her in my little-kid way. Mom and Dad never came back, but Grandma hated her daughter, liked her dumbass son-in-law even less, said it was a blessing to be rid of the goddamn moochers, and I agreed. We moved house a couple of times, Grandma saying it would make it harder for them to find us, if they did come back, though probably the real reason was she was always behind in the rent.

Grandma was an experienced shoplifter and taught me all the tricks. We even worked up a team act: I'd go in first, looking innocent, grab something, and stroll out with it like I thought it was freebie day in the supermarket, setting off a ruckus that usually involved giving me a piece of candy to retrieve the goods, while Grandma kept busy behind their backs, checking off her grocery list. It was how we put dinner on the table, until we ran out of supermarkets and big delis with their strategic aisles. It was bad luck to hit the same address twice, as Grandma used to say, two being mostly an unlucky number in her scheme of things. So, we moved on to drug stores and then to department stores, which were best of all. Sometimes the clerks seemed almost to help us, turning their backs at just the right moment, even suggesting, under the guise of a sales pitch, items we should include in our loot. They probably hated their jobs, were getting back at their skinflint owners. Snagged my favorite Mad Monsters tee that way. Doesn't fit anymore, but it's still in my dirty socks bag.

When I was little, Grandma rocked me in her rocking chair and played with my weewee, as she called it. Said she was casting a spell on it to make it grow big. Probably not a proper thing to do, but it felt good. A little like getting your bare back scratched when it's itchy. Climbed up on her lap long after I was too big to do that. Not anymore. I came home one day to find her sitting up stiff in her rocker, starting to go off, eyes crossed, and jaw hanging open like she'd croaked of a last heehaw. I thought she was playing a nasty trick on me. Felt resentful. Haven't completely gotten over it.

Cookie, black cigarette dangling off his lower lip, fires up the oven. He's clumsily unwrapping and heating up the first pass-arounds by the time a trio of musicians arrives, led by an ugly fat man carrying a beat-up tenor sax case. The other two zone in on a stand-up bass and a glossy fancyass piano with a lyre on its nameplate in the den next door. Nice piece of gear, I noticed it as soon as we arrived, though I wondered at the time how they got it up here. And *in* here. Did they have to take it apart and rebuild it, or did they build this penthouse around it? Too big to pocket, but I appreciate quality when I see it. Probably even the nameplate can be hocked.

The sax player comes over to cadge a drink while I'm still laying things out, saying he needs to moisten the reeds, and I ask him what he's getting paid. "No idea, man, but not enough," he wheezes. "Anyways, no real music tonight, just fucken room-fill with a coupla goofballs I never seen before. So, craft me something potent, boy, to help me hack through it." The barman shrugs and twists the cap off a whiskey bottle, pours me one over ice. Scrawny punk, hiding it behind a goatee and sideburns, a surly cool. Probably digs nothing but loud noise, the big beat. Which I can do, but only as a table-setter. Storm before the calm.

Nearly forgot this gig. I was in a sleazy inner city gyp-joint, jamming with a dreadlocked geek in there who whacked furiously at the house piano, and hoping someone might stand us a drink, even if only to shut us up, when I suddenly remembered I had a job tonight. Couldn't recall the details, like what I was getting paid, for example, but these have been hard times in the music bizz, can't turn anything down, so I hurried outside and grabbed a cab, the keyboard maestro inviting himself along. The cabbie let us off at a mile-high building, and, following the little signs, we took the elevator to the penthouse up here at the top, where we found a sullen string of bones slouching under a mop of silky hair in the entrance hall. He didn't say anything, just followed us in as though he'd been waiting for us. Neither of us knew him. I smiled at him just to piss him off. Turned out by luck he was a bassist. He didn't have a strat, but we found one inside, and a monster grand for young Dreads as well. So, suddenly it's a trio. Cool. *My* trio.

Last time I headlined a combo was more than a decade ago, percussionist and plug-in keyboard as my sides, midtown venue, dark and juicy. The percussionist was gifted in a freaky sort of way, slapping softly at a parade of skins with a mesmerizing thuckety-thuck-thuck, while blowing or shaking a wide range of kooky instruments from whistleflutes and posthorns to a glass harmonica and rainsticks, getting everybody moving collectively as one body. But the guy on the souped-up ivories was one of a kind, a fucking genius. I always looked down on wired keyboards as a kind of toy, until I heard him riff on one. I was mainly an archetypal dance-on-the-bar screamer and honker back then, honking not only a tool to cover up all the boners, but also a route into what I thought of as the Emptiness. It was a state of mind that scared the shit out of me most of the time, but when I was locked in, walking on the spot and bleating away, I felt at one with the universe. Which is also empty. Mindless. Wanted to just disappear into it. Nirvana, man. The young crowd loved it. But at the time, I had to tame my act to synch with the resident hotshot, take up a quieter agenda. The wiry little man sometimes spent ages, hovering over the keys before tentatively touching one of them, and then he'd burst into a sudden melodic solo run that left us all breathless.

I was just dicking around on my own one afternoon in a darkened bar, raucously booting a few all-caps brass blurts on my horn as a way of blotting out the silence, when the keyboard whiz turned up out of nowhere on a shadowy barstool in there. He told me, his voice echoey in the vacated bar, that my workout was pretty wild, but it wasn't wild enough. He asked me what I could do with a single note, so I showed him, it being right down honkers' alley, and he grunted and said he liked it, it was provocative, but still not crazy enough. You got to drive through the pyros, he said, to find the nut on the other side. Didn't know what that was, but I trusted him. I'd always suspected there was something more there, I'd felt it out at the edge before, and now I began to work seriously at reaching it. First time, really,

I'd ever worked at anything. I had a genuine audience cheering me on—only of one, but one who could listen with both his ears, not merely a gang of frenzied weed-stunned kids. And he knew how to make room for me, open up a lead, let me flex. Our trio even got famous for a time as a kind of sweet and sour combo, grounded by the dreamy percussionist with the soft palms, but, hard as I tried, I couldn't break through to the magic I could sense just beyond my horn.

It all came abruptly to an end. Fame turned out to be a real downer for the keyboard artist, who claimed it warped his spine around and drove it straight up his ass, and one day, just as we were drawing up new contracts for real money, he staggered out on us, clutching his butt with both hands as if it were about to blow out its contents. I realized that I'd been discipling a lunatic, and that what I was trying to break through to was plain madness. The contracts were canceled. My trio was canceled. There might have been other gigs to be had, but I didn't want them. Hit the skids after that, sucked up too much hooch, dilapidated myself. Bad time, only dimly remembered.

Finally, my empty pockets and emptier belly cast me back into my old bread-and-butter routines, screaming and honking, not for breakthroughs, but for nickels and dimes. I found I'd been missing the routines, where they took me. Honking's not such a big deal anymore, the frenetic kids have new obsessions, but I'm home again. Most of the bands don't trust me, associating me with the wacky keyboarder and recalling my own drop-out weirdness, so work has been hard to find. Have had to take cheap stints with start-up dance bands, play saxophone tunes for junior high school proms, or do private parties like this one, become a tootler. And all the time, that crazy virtuoso, wherever he was, has had me by the goolies with his nutty dream, has had me blowing my brains out, trying to blast through to the far side. Find the silence: last thing he said to me. Which I heard as: find the Emptiness.

Honking doesn't really go with this cushy décor, and there's no way I could crawl up on that bar and stomp about in my old way without falling off, but I feel like something might work out up here tonight. In the piano room, where we'll have to assemble our trio, there are no dimmers on the lights, but the bulbs can be screwed out or smashed. Kicking out the lights could be part of the act. I've been waiting for an incendiary breakthrough, and I can feel it. Like a tingle in the cock. Tonight, I'll get there. I can do it.

The caterer comes by with a platter of seared scallops topped with black caviar, and, sampling a bite herself, offers me one. Wasn't hungry. Now I am. She reminds me of a chick who gave me head between sets, years ago, this one an older filled-out version, attractive in a beat-up way, a bit fat, but what the hell, I'm fat and beat-up, too. And feeling celebrative: tonight's the night. I ask her if she can sing, maybe we can make a little music together. "You know," I growl with a snarky sort of grin, black fish eggs staining his broken teeth, "a star is born and all that jazz." I tell him I can carry a tune, if it doesn't have more notes than "Mary Had a Little Lamb." He laughs a wheezy laugh and says, "Hey, girl, let's go find Mary's flockin' sheep!" "They ain't lost," I say.

Actually I've had a career, but I don't tell the sleazebag that. The whole routine: agent, recording contracts, sweet swing quartet to sing with, soft mazy nights, money that came and went, a life that came and went with it. I was young and skinny then, still in my teens. There was a drummer in that quartet, good-looking, funny in a deadpan sort of way, a bit wild, and on the needle. Something he taught me. I was a fast learner. End of career. During rehab, my voice plummeted and lost its sweet overtones, gigs were hard to come by, and, in my misery, I was soon shooting up again. By that time, the drummer was in the looney bin, didn't know me when I went to see him, both of us losers in the end, though he was probably crazy long before we got it on. One night, while we were still together, I asked him why he never smiled, even when telling a joke, and he told me about the old unshaven addict who raped him. His father. Said his old man couldn't stop laughing, while all the time slapping his kid's ass and driving away. If he'd had a blade, he said, he would have orphaned himself on the spot. Hasn't put on a happy face since. I was sorry I'd asked.

This sax man is a loser, too, but he doesn't look like a junkie. Just a bloated drunk in loud clothes with a battered horn. Doesn't smell all that good either. Lots of ways to lose. The other two music hires are on some kind of cheap high—weed, coke, speed, maybe all at once. The longhair opening his double bass box is a mean sort, lanky, droopy-eyed, wasted. Probably coddling a thick lazy dick too big for his pants. World-hater. The pianist with the greasy dreads curtaining his acne might be more interesting. Or, shades of my drummer, he might be a total nut-case. Can't stop bobbing about like his butt's on fire. What the drummer taught me with his body was connection, with his craziness disconnection. Or maybe it was the other way around. Sad story, either way. But still carrying the torch. Memories of sweet nights: what one's left with.

That and a lot of pain, a lot of emptiness. It settles on me like a black cloud sometimes, and not much helps to lift it off, except howling out. When, as a kid, I fell into the dumps, I sang with the church choir. Didn't buy in to the crazy kiddie tales that all the fat ladies like my Mom orgasmed over, rest in peace, but I bawled out the gospel songs like a true believer and they wailed along with me and, next thing I knew, I was out of church and into nightclubs, singing with the quartet, bedding down with the drummer. Happy for the first time in my life.

One night, our veins bouncing with horse, but on the nod and feeling dreamy, the rush's high a distant memory, the drummer switched disks from the usual big-beat mattress music to something sweetly but melancholically highbrow, a knock-turn, as he called it. He crawled inside me and I fell asleep, and maybe he did, too, though he wasn't in my dream-thoughts. Nothing was, really. I was afloat in a soft gray wordlessness. A sad hollow voice was asking questions, but they were not questions that had to be answered, only listened to sympathetically, as you would listen to a sick child you were rocking. Someone or something vaguely dangerous walked past in the dark, but the child assured me, just by being there, that everything was going to be all right. And for a short time—too short a time, but more than I'd ever imagined possible—it was. More than all right. It was fantastic. Then, life said, fuck you; its teasing prelims were over.

I woke up one morning, dumbed down to nothing and sick as a bitch, on the sidewalk outside the Grange—the Grunge, as the regulars call it—a miserable little two-bit eatery on the wrong side of town. My side. Used to be, decades ago, a charity kitchen for country kids, lost in the big city. That's me. Went in to cop a mug of black java, and got hired on the cheap by Cookie, only name I know him by, a crippled migrant deep-fat fryer, one staggering step from the crazy house. Tonight, though, under his puffy chef's bonnet, he has crispened up, turning out amazing foolyou-tays, sesame rammin' cakes, roasted oysters and eggy things with lobster, flicking the dials on the shiny new digital oven like he's been doing it all his life. His old grease-caked iron stove in the Grunge, by contrast, looks like a relic from some wartime mess hall of the last century. Best I can understand Cookie's broken English, that wretched chophouse he runs was a gift from a sister who worked the local streets and maybe is no more. Or maybe it wasn't a gift. Maybe it wasn't a sister. The dude's legs don't work, but he has big strong hands, snaky eyes.

He didn't remember the billet he had, but then he did. Fat money, he said, and handed me a note ripped from the phone pad. We grabbed up a couple of armloads of plastic and paper, Cookie found some house jug wine, we threw together some ham sandwiches, boxed it all up, kicked the bums out, shut down the Grunge, and jumped in the house van, a filthy old rattler with stacks of folding tables and chairs in the back. Or anyway I jumped, he crawled. I couldn't read the address on the phone-pad scrap, nor could Cookie, he couldn't even say for sure that it was his own handwriting, but he said he knew where we were going. High-in-sky, he said, the flat singsong way you'd say pigs-in-blankets. He could hardly walk, I thought he might ask me to drive, but he parked one of his filthy black cigarettes between his thick lips and commandeered the driver's seat. We ripped round and round in tire-screeching circles, Cookie driving like a pissed-off maniac, but we ended up here, just the same. Luckily, we found a young hood leaning on the front gate, joint dangling from his loose lips, and Cookie talked him into helping us carry everything up in exchange for working the bar, which the kid said was his specialty. As it turned out, we could have left it all back at the shop; this classy spread was already laid out for us. The street-boy is cute in a dippy way with his funny chin whiskers, and I sometimes feel a convulsive little fanny flutter around him, like something has got inside me and is slithering around, but it's probably only hunger. Stomach's been growling like a lioness in heat.

I peek under the shiny lids of our dining-room chafers (they're heavy, must be solid silver, or else plated castiron), and in one of them there are herbed lamb lollipops. Can't resist. I'm just sneaking a bite when the first guest turns up, way too early, looking confused. He *is* confused. "Is it already over?" he asks, peering around in alarm through his thick smeared specs. Frayed black suit, likely the only one he owns; might have been a tux once upon a time. Wrinkled white shirt, clip-on black bowtie, wild fringe of dirty white hair around his pink ears, a few dark threads pasted across the top. Probably a freeloader cruising buffets. I hold up one of the lollypops. "No, you're just in time, pops," the woman says with a wink, and offers me one of the black balls on a bent stick she's chewing on. "First customer of the night!"

I mutter a desperate no-thank-you and flee to the family bar. "A glass of water," I tell the young man in there. "With ice, please." Have I come to the wrong place? Nothing in my pockets. I must have left the invitation in my room. But it feels right to be here. The owners have money, maybe they're patrons of the arts, aware of my importance to the development of world music. In fact, wasn't Mrs. What's-her-name, the owner's wife, once a student of mine?

I walk the water over to a painting taking up most of the back wall, if it's not just the wallpaper, and adopt a thoughtful

OPEN HOUSE

expression, pretending I can actually see it (a still life? contorted human figure? a falling building?). What else can you do when you're at a party and no one else is there? Maybe I should go out and come back in again. It wouldn't be the first time I've had to do that. I was once invited to conduct a program that included one of my own groundbreaking masterpieces, and it was felt that only I could properly interpret it. Meaning: no one else understood it. I walked onstage, rapped my baton vigorously on the lectern, raised my arms and, with a flamboyant gesture meant to awe the audience, called for the opening crash of orchestral dissonance—but was met with silence, then scattered laughter and applause. An imbecilic protest by neo-Romantics? No, it was my fault. I had seen an orchestra that wasn't there, they were still filing in. The whole auditorium erupted in whinnying laughter. I had no choice but to leave the stage and, when assured all the players were seated, reenter. Scowling, of course, which got another laugh. I had a bit of a reputation as a comedian after that and was asked to repeat the routine at the next concert. Maybe, instead of snapping back in rage, I should have done so.

I was a formidable figure back then, my rigorous twelve-tone compositions serialism's gold standard. Students wrote their doctoral theses on my sequences, and my intimidatingly complex scores were fine-tooth-combed the way runes once were by the kabbalists in their search for secret oracles. There was hardly a concert, anywhere in the world, that did not include a work of mine. Knotty, my music was called, gritty, pungent with dissonance. And indispensable. Other composers either adopted our serial procedures, or were booed out of the concert halls by loyal students. We were known as the serialist bullies for daring to believe passionately in a different kind of music. Admittedly, we could be uncompromising, some would say cruel, and a few insignificant careers were ruined, but we were alone in an ignorant and hostile world, making something new. There was a price to pay.

There had always been something harshly atonal about my music, but in the early days it moved rigidly down a linear path toward climax, its implicit anger nestled snugly in the bars and lines of the omnipresent stave. I didn't ask where the stave came from, how it acquired the authority that it had, but then one day I did. The result was my first true breakaway piece: "The Stave Is Gone." Much more important was "Answering the Dodecaphone," written for string quartet and triangle that same feverish year, but it's almost unplayable (when the lead violinist complained about that in an interview, we saw to it that his entire quartet was dismissed), so "The Stave Is Gone" is what has stuck and, though trivial, defines me to this day. In fact, it was still being played a year or two ago, though admittedly that was mainly because an animated film used a tone row from it as the track for one of its cat-and-mouse chases.

By the time of the breakthrough, I was at the Academy, teaching music composition as a mathematical science, as has been done ever since the Enlightenment; but mathematics had evolved, while the Academy was still mired in the Arithmetic Age. Too many tenured old fogies, clinging to power. I wasted a lot of time as chair stripping them of that power, pushing them into early retirement, fighting to incorporate dodecaphony into the curriculum, along with string theory, all the new digital media, set theory—but what good did it do? The sentimental tonalists are back, a new generation of them, more stupid and powerful than ever, destroying all we created.

Now, orchestras and soloists alike shun my compositions, calling them "unmusical," purposelessly difficult. Why can't I write "ordinary" music, they want to know? The fools. Vanguard music that was once universally admired as cutting-edge is scoffed at today as we once scoffed at the traditionalists, my own life's work dismissed as a passing fancy. Everyone's back into tonality now, prostituting themselves with lyricism and egregious harmonies in a vain effort to win back audiences too ignorant to appreciate the simple fact that harmony is a lie in a disharmonious world. Meanwhile, the New Music lies dead. Assassinated by mad Christians and other nonmusical ruffians.

Aha. Maybe *that's* the piece I've been struggling to write for the past decade, the new thing I must finish before I die: the operatic tale of the murder of a heroic form. Can a form be a hero? Of course, it can! While musing about that, I seem to hear three bell-like notes. They sound over and over, as though to impress upon me their urgency. I recognize them, they're the first three notes of a classical overture that I once borrowed for a famous parody. There was a three-word note taped to the entrance door, bold enough for me to read with my nose pressed against it, and the sequence seems to be singing them, as though the phrase in its clarity and purity were asking to title the work. Maybe I'm imagining the notes, or maybe they're real, but—good grief, they *are* real! They're the *door chimes!* Crowds are pouring in! I can tell by the vapidity of their clamor that these people are musical illiterates. Will they even know who I am? I avoid them by slipping into the next room where the mocking chimes are less intrusive.

A little jazz group is warming up in here. I have occasionally used jazz elements in my compositions, have worked with musicians like these. I walk up to the tall angular man unpacking a double bass, but before I can even introduce myself, the nasty fellow spits at me and turns his back. There's a muscular young woman with long twisty pigtails (the owner's daughter?) sitting at the grand piano, banging away like a child having a tantrum, and a corpulent gentleman is using his saxophone as a kind of sonic weapon. I approach the saxophonist deferentially when he pauses for a breath, and I remark, one musician to another, that I once heard a jazz piece for four saxophones, using the twelve-tone method, but can't recall the composer. Has he heard of it? He rolls his eyes and releases an uncivil blast on his saxophone that drives me from the room into the kitchen.

I fill my empty water glass at the kitchen tap, my hands trembling. Who are these people? The world grows uglier by the hour! The windows over the sink look out on what is apparently a roof terrace, still bathed in an early evening glow. Wait! Aren't I supposed to give a lecture on the New Music out there? It's why I'm here, for God's sake! I seem to have left my notes at home, but no matter, I've been a teacher all my life, and the topic's *my* topic. Those three classic notes are still ringing, an urgent call muffled now by the shouted banalities. I could start with that sequence as an introduction to my new work-in-progress, with its ironic title of the three words they've just seen on the door, each syllable dominated by a nasal hum, then tell them how the piece will open the door to a deeper understanding of serialism, and thus of my own oeuvre within it. It may be the most difficult and, at the same time, most accessible thing he has ever written, they will say. Ingenious! I'm getting excited about it. If it weren't for the nuisance of this lecture, I'd get started immediately.

On a counter near the door out to the terrace, there's an old cello lying on its back. I lower my face to it, and discover it's an eighteenth century Montagnana—just carelessly dropped there! The vulgar power of the rich! Pressing my ear to the strings, one of them seems to sound by itself. Is it trying to speak to me? Letting me know what I must tell these ignorant fools? I borrow the cello and step out onto the terrace, moving toward what looks like a lectern and microphone, but that turns out to be just a tall bushy plant. Are there any people out here? Over there, somebody squatting in the bushes: *a naked woman!* What is she *doing?* No, wait, she's only a statue, must be—*What?* Did she just *move?* Oh my god! Why have I come *out* here? He wheels around, but finds the door locked, bangs on it in panic. Not many things make me happy. This makes me happy. Perhaps the old fart senses me watching, for he backs off, looking confused and guilty. He *is* guilty, and not only for stealing that museum piece— he's the tyrannical half-blind old cunt who got me thrown out of music school, ruined my career. Ruined my life! I owe him one.

No sign yet of the hosts, but the mob's rolling in. There's a note taped to the front door that says, COME ON IN! I'd have taken it down and locked the door, but paying gigs don't fall in your lap every day. They've read the sign and have been doing that, all the squealing little piggies, they've come wallowing on in. At first just a few, then more and more, shouting, laughing, giving themselves names, wave after wave of them. Except for the married ones, it's not clear they know each other, though right away they're working on it. Maybe the marrieds don't know each other either. Sooner or later, they'll unlock the back door and swarm out onto the roof terrace, so it's time for a quick rescue operation. He's too blind to recognize me, I'll have to tell him who his savior is . . .

Back inside, there's a buxom lady waiting for me. I ignore her, light up some weed, advertising the junk for sale in my pocket, and hunker down in the piano room behind the voluptuous ass-end of my double bass. The lady refuses to be ignored. She tells me she saw what I did. Shit, I'm thinking, maybe she ought to follow the old composer, but there are crowds now out on the terrace, so I offer her some money instead. All that I'm earning tonight. She refuses it. It's probably too little, but I don't have any more. I start to cry, more out of frustration than anything like anguish. She sees what she assumes to be my pain, asks more about the old guy. I build him up as an incorrigible individualist and egomaniac, concerned only for himself at the expense of everyone else, and she says that defensive actions, when accompanied by an intransigent moral ruthlessness, are sometimes necessary, no matter how extreme, to counter the obscene lack of discipline in contemporary culture. I'm not sure what she's talking about, but it seems like the wily bitch has bought my line. She says that we must move beyond mere cavil, find other like-minded persons. Her use of "we" lets me know that she has plans for me, provided I pledge allegiance to her. No choice. But none wanted. I think I can get on with her, at least until I figure out how to get rid of her. She leaves me to think about all that, and goes off to round up others.

I badly need a beer, but I haven't had my hands on a double bass since music school, and if what I need right now is relaxation, I'm as apt to find it with this beauty as with a beer. Haven't met the two stoned dipshits I'm apparently booked with, if "booked" is the word—a fat old-fashioned sax honker and a keyboard guy sporting dreadlocks, who clearly believes a piano has to be bludgeoned into submission, no matter what its lineage—

so we'll have to fake the plot. If I don't like their music, I'll play my own. There's a bow on a chair nearby, but bowings are no longer part of my fucking repertoire; I thumb a few warm-up notes, keep my head down. The new arrivals, still piling in, glance around, make a quick read of the scene, grab up drinks and plates of food, carry them around like stage props. Oddly, there's a nun among them, wearing a white cornette and monastic scapular, looking piously relaxed in spite of her freakish dress.

Curious, that nun arriving so soon after I did what I did, but I keep my eyes off her, try to (is she staring at me?), centering instead on the slope-shouldered sweetheart pressed against my knees. This lady was waiting for me when we arrived, as I had a feeling she would be. She seems almost to play herself, and, even when plucking her, the sound she makes is more like the stroke of a horsehair bow. Weird, but nice. Earthy tones, almost menacing, ghostly, yet alluring. Gut strings, too, easier on the fingers. The character who crafted this beauty has signed the ornamental scroll near the pegbox, not with his name, but with a command: LOVE ME. I do, man.

My last year in high school, my classmates were all trying to get into one university or another, but I hated books, so I braced myself for trade school and a shitty life, eased by dope. Luckily, my biology teacher, funny little guy with a wiry tuft of gray hair under his nose, heard me plinking a fiddle with an amateur folk group. I just picked it up, I said when he asked. Great natural talent, he said, you should be in music school. He offered to cover the tuition, switched me to the double bass, paid for the lessons he said I'd need to get through the school auditions. I was so fucking innocent, I thought it was from a genuine admiration of my talent and the goodness of his heart. Well, any skill can be learned, even blow jobs. I flunked the first audition, was ready to give it up, but the pianist the teacher had hired to prep me was one tough bitch. When she thought I hadn't practiced enough, she pulled my pants down and used a braided leather riding crop on my exposed ass. The teacher might have stopped her, but all he did was watch. I passed the second audition, scared not to.

I had to thank the sadists, though. Music school was the most beautiful thing that ever happened to me. I'd been an outsider all my life and suddenly I *belonged* to something. That magical first day, I joined everything—the orchestra, chamber ensembles, trios, jazz and folk groups, whoever'd have me, even the chess club and the bowling team. I was, in short, in love—with a god-damn institution, no less! Hah! I *hate* institutions! That big double bass was an awkward mother to lug around, but I took her with me everywhere. The other students seemed to love it when I plucked a few pizz notes on her. She had that melancholic thumpy sound of the old 78s. Sex bomb. Life was beginning to make sense, even if it was all an illusion.

But then the conservatory took a dark turning. I hadn't been there a year when the great classical tradition began to be shouted down from within by a gang of rebellious noise-makers, taking over the school in a naked power grab, that autocrat out on the roof terrace among them. Serialism, my own conservatory professor explained, was just a wobble in music history, a momentarily dangerous substitution of mathematics for feeling. Can't take it seriously. Listening to the music they write is like suffering a mental breakdown. I sided with him against the pretentious shits who were taking over the Academy, but, within a month or two, the shits had won and my prof was being forcibly retired, looking suddenly like a very tired old man.

I soon followed him to the exit, but without his cushion of retirement checks: I was unceremoniously kicked out, accused of stealing school instruments. They were only guessing; they realized they'd made a mistake accepting me in the first place, saw me as a trouble-maker, pal of the faculty deadbeats, and used the alleged thefts as an excuse to expel me. And they were just cheap out-of-tune school instruments, the whole lot worth less at the pawn shops than the antique my accuser just stole. Cost me school, degree, career. Word of the accusations followed me around, kept me out of other music schools. What I was left with was a bitter hatred. Hated the school, the music they played, hated even the classics I'd loved (those bastards didn't defend me as they should have), a hatred that spread to all the ugly art works in the museums and galleries, the shapeless lumps passing for sculpture, the crappy plays in all the theaters, even the over-hyped movies playing on screens everywhere. I was full of fury, fed on it.

Time for that beer. I set the lady on her stand, stub out the maryjane, raise a middle finger to the honking sax player, and, elbows out, push into the room with a bar in it, eye out for the buxom lady. I catch a glimpse of the roof terrace: I was right, the crowds have already shoved on out there. Not sure what made me do that, but it felt right at the time, necessary even. Like there was something in the air, an endorsement of sorts. Where was the lady standing? Well, no regrets. It'll work out. The goateed bartender is under a lot of pressure, but he's cool, taking his time with each pour, paying little attention to who's next in line, while scouting the swarm for chicks he can hit on. He spies me deep in the pack-up and tosses me a cold beer. It's picked off by a young smartass in an incandescent golden tee with a string tie knotted around his bare throat, but the barkeep flashes a grin and pitches me another.

"Hey, *I'm* next," protests a toothy hawkfaced broad with orange hair, a smoke between her teeth, pushing forward as I'm squeezing past, going the other way. Not what the man is looking for, and beaknose senses that. "Anything with gin in it, buster," she snaps. The barguy picks up two pitchers, a green one and a pink one. He's a pompous twit with his fruity little goatee, but just a boy, I could be his mother. I wink and point at the pink one, not really caring what's in it, any shit'll do. Some bitch laughs shrilly and a nearby dude grunts like his balls have been grabbed. Real estate would be a happy career, if it weren't for the buyers and sellers. True of everything of course.

What's buzzing through my wrecked mind is the root question: whose party is this? Very upscale piece of real estate. Chief cook, barguy, jazz trio, amazing hors d'oeuvres and free booze, chafers filling up with haut cuisine, a ritzy show. How did I get invited? No help to be had from the inrushing babble; mostly strangers, jammed butt-to-butt, and more pushing through the doors with the impatience of mutts in heat. The noisome racket recalls the flatulent idiocy of sales conferences, or else drunken farewell parties for departing pals. *Hang on!* Is that it? Are the owners going somewhere? Selling off? Is this an open house? Could be why I'm here, though I don't remember scheduling it. Wait, maybe I do. Fuzzily. Gotta lay off the daytime juice.

The barguy seems to have his eye on a jade statuette nonchalantly showing off her slim nakedness on a shelf at one end of the bar. She's cute. Reminds me of that wispy girl with the tiny breasts and lean little teenage butt. As she was then. Still is probably, except for the tits. I scan the crowd, looking for possible owners of this posh squat. Maybe they're out on their roof terrace, getting away from all the ganja fumes. It's my job to check if that's why I'm here, but I'm reluctant to stray too far from the bar. Across the room, a hustler with a thick salt-and-paprika beard, huddled under a ruined fedora, is trying to weasel a giddy fat woman into something. An old con artist merely on the lookout for a fast lay, or another realtor, out to steal my clients? With his eerie gap-toothed smile, he doesn't look smart enough for either.

The jade statuette maintains its cool insouciance. I should, too. I feel lovingly chastised.

They were getting married and looking for a home. He was older with deep pockets, handsome in a badboy sort of way, bit of a boor, given to dumb jokes about marital woes, she a cute kid, somewhat tittery, clearly nervous about the decision she'd made. I gave them a tour of available properties, the girl very interested, he not at all. He seemed in fact merely to be indulging her, as though he'd already made up his mind. He had. The bride-to-be scheduled another tour for a second look at properties that had appealed to her the first time around, but she came alone. I pressed her and she confessed that it was too late, her fiancé had already bid on another property, but she thought of me as a kind of big sister, and needed my advice.

I probably should have turned it off right there, sorting out boy-girl problems are not my line of work, but she was such a sweet child, so vulnerable, so naïve, and the guy such a dick-head, that I decided to hear her out. It took a while, her account full of embarrassed stops and starts—she was so much in love, he was such a nice man, and he loved her so, doted on her really, she trusted him entirely, etc. We started over coffee, and it was in the café smoking room that she timidly revealed that the apartment her future husband was acquiring was next door to where his most recent wife was now living. I knew the address. Gated community, very private, properties changing hands without the involvement of estate agents. She didn't know what was planned for their wedding night, but she was afraid it might involve his ex. "Uh oh," I said. "Time to duck out."

I asked her if she knew why he and the first wife split. "Well, she wasn't the first," she said shyly, waving away my smoke. "But probably it was because his, you know, his thingie, somehow got bent. Sideways." I started to snort. Not very big sisterish, but I couldn't stop myself. "It's not really funny," she said, in a tone more of appeal than admonishment. Then, in a whisper: "When it goes in you, it sometimes sort of hurts."

"Oh no!" I whooped. The others in the café were turning toward us, expectant grins on their faces. I did what I could to convert my snorts into a cough, mashed out the smoke, dropped some cash on the table. "Let's go for a drive," I said, still working on the fake cough.

By the time we parked on a bluff overlooking the pricey part of town, I wouldn't say I was in love yet, but I was definitely developing a crush. In that whispery little girl's voice, she described the traction device that her stud was using to try to straighten out his cock, explaining that the reason she couldn't even think about leaving him was because he needed her help putting it on. "It presses the head of his thingie into what looks like the bill of a bathtub duck," she said without a hint of a smile, and I lost it again, my hand playfully slapping her thigh as I haplessly woof-woofed—whereupon she fell, sobbing, on my shoulder. And then I did fall in love, loving everything about her, her winsome naiveté, her piteous boohooing on her big sister's shoulder, her little upturned nose, so unlike my own schnoz, her pretty peek-aboo breasts, and, maybe most of all, her tight little cheeks, by then in my grip, my fingers searching between them.

She said she was really sorry for taking up my time, but her fiancé had asked her to get breast implants and she didn't know how to say no. That sobered me up and I pulled my hand away—then quickly put it back again, now in a more big-sisterly way. I told her she didn't want to do that, and she agreed, snuggling closer, shifting her bottom under my hand. She was crying. "I'm scared," she whimpered. I gave her buns a little squeeze and told her to stay scared, her breasts were perfect, don't let anyone mess with them! "You're just saying that to be nice," she said in her sweet little-girl voice, her eyes brimming with tears. Then she pulled away, still snuffling, glanced at her watch, and said she really hated to leave me, but she had to get back to her apartment; she was making supper for him and a few friends to prove she could. I didn't want to take her home, but did, arguing all the way against the implants, and, before waving goodbye, she leaned inside the car and kissed me. "Thank you so much for everything," she whispered. "You're my best friend ever!"

When she didn't call, I was afraid that was it. I mostly just sat at my desk, moaning and breaking pencils. The real estate bizz was out the window, I could think of nothing but that girl and her sweet ass—*snap!*

Then suddenly she did call, asking me to come to her apartment. Right away. "You were so helpful!" I hadn't realized how hard I'd fallen until I heard her silly voice. I took a shower, aromatized the bod, ran a comb through my hair for the first time in a week, swept the broken pencil stubs into a wastebasket, brushed my teeth, pulled on a dress and silk panties, then took off the underpants. I ached to have my hands on her ass again, to lick her pointy little breasts, and, above all, to get my snout down there between her thighs, the one thing it's good for. On the drive over, I rehearsed opening lines, imagined her greeting me by falling deliriously into my arms.

She met me at the door, smiling idiotically, with her blouse off. Her huge phony boobs flopped obscenely. "What have you *done*, you stupid cow?" I shrieked.

"Please don't be angry! I told him no way, just like you said, but his friends talked him into it! And it's OK, I *am* more beautiful! They all *said* so!" She was dumping me! I could hear it in her infantile whimper, see it on her traitorous face. "I thought you'd *like* them when you saw them, like everyone else does!" I was starting to bawl. Not the coolest thing I do: I launch great wheezing gasps that would scare the pants off anyone. "I'll call a doctor!" she yelped and slammed the door. Game over.

I drink off the pink thing and ask the barguy for another. "Any goddamn color," I say, lighting up. There's a boy in a classy black chamois jacket, promising, but he's too young unless his daddy's loaded. Another in pressed bluejeans looks spoiled but he probably owns fewer banknotes than I do. That bearded con artist in the soft battered lid, on the other hand, is now hustling a handsome dude who's been casing the property, taking video notes. Tailored suit, loosened tie, shoes freshly shined. Man with money. Fashionably eccentric: no socks. He bypasses the booze, his mind on something else. Is he thinking of dropping a bid? Worth a shot. "Hey," I call out. "Just a minute—!" I turn to flee. A termagant with her head on fire is bearing down on me, seemingly intent on pitching this apartment to me. To avoid both her and the overly inquisitive philosophe with the wagging facehair who's been grilling me, I squeeze through the congestion into a room full of witless inebriates, looking for a safe place to hide.

Where am I? No idea. I ask the cellphone I found in a lady's handbag to locate me, but the app seems not to be working. The altitude maybe. The pictures I've been taking aren't there either, only the ones loaded by the previous owner. I flick through them, eye out for pornographic images sick enough to coax her into buying back this dysfunctional rubbish—pictures of the lady herself, say, masturbating with a loaded revolver, or an indiscreet hubby or lover cavorting in girls' panties, even naked children in the bathtub or under a garden hose—but nothing. Power-point lectures, ghastly meetings, market reports: a business woman, more attentive to finance than to her little prayer-niche. In short, a bore.

I pocket the phone and, leaning back against the wall, I ask a cute young chick how she found out about the party. "Through a friend," she says. "She told me she was going to a wild blow-out, and invited me along." I ask her if the party has lived up to her expectations. "Oh yes, it's loads of fun . . ." "It was the light that drew us up here," says an edgy lady in wire-rimmed spectacles. "All the floors below were dark." Really? How did I miss that . . . ? A third, a chatty little fellow with yellow slicked-back hair, believes he knows the people who live here and may have received a phone invitation. "I was at a party here some years ago. After the theater, maybe. Nice soaks, I mean folks. Heh heh." Others say they heard party sounds overhead as they walked past, just "following our own feet," and decided to check them out. "A sign on the door said, 'Come on in,' so we did," said a member of a female gang of tough teenagers, elbowing their way now toward the food chafers. Some simply don't know, just felt an obscure obligation. My experience precisely. I have a hunch how things play out here, but not yet how to turn a profit from it.

A huge woman, reeking of cheap perfume and wearing a childish lilac bow in her permed hair, waddles up, gushing about the jazz trio, so I slip away into the next room where those wretched musicians are at work, violating some innocent song. Or maybe they're banging away at a gang of three different songs, all at the same time. Travesty, in either case. The bassist, head down over his busy knuckles, offers me something at a special price, an antique cello, if I heard him right. Evidently, a redistributor of private goods like myself. I ask him how much, but his concealed reply is drowned out by the bleating saxophonist and his hammer-fisted pianist, the incessant rattle of empty laughter and the high-decibel yatter, so I keep moving, wondering why it is I'm not wearing socks. Also wondering who owns this classy but ethereal property, and realizing, as I squeeze from room to room through the blended party smoke, that others are wondering much the same thing, though with less sobriety, less percipience. Their faces are becoming familiar to me in an untagged generic way, and I pause to pick a pocket or two, learning more as I do so about their identities, their confusions. One of them compliments me on "my" chef's exquisite feuilletons and lobster frittatas, evidently assuming that I'm responsible for this spread, so when the beaked realtor collars me at last, I ask her what she thinks my property is worth.

"What? You mean, you own this place?" she gasps, staring at me incredulously. The stupid woman is almost too drunk to stand, but she can still be used. There's a desk in here. Must be an office. I stare back coldly at her and tell her my price. "Good grief! Isn't that a bit . . . over the top?"

"It's very unusual," I reply icily. "Where are you going to find another like it? But I'll need the entire amount in cash—*tonight!*"

"Oh no! You're not leaving—?"

"The old story, conniving woman in collusion with the law, I have to skip town immediately. I'll listen to offers, but I trust you to find the entire amount. There are rich people here for whom that sum is pocket change. You can keep a third of whatever you dig out of them."

She sobers up quickly. "I'll need the title . . . "

"Yes, of course, it's in the wall-safe here in my office." I rattle some keys of uncertain provenance in her face, and point vaguely behind me, hoping there's a safe somewhere back there. "You have about thirty minutes."

There's an altercation in the next room. The bartender has slugged a gentleman with elegant white handlebars, who was apparently offended by the careless *glug-glug* pouring of a thirty-year-old claret. It *was* offensive. I take the opportunity to berate the bartender as any proper owner would, not for striking the elderly guest, but for failing to show due respect to the aged wine. The bartender nods, catching my drift, and mumbles an apology, allowing he must have misread the label. It seems I have a knack for the proprietor's role. The white-mustachioed gent with the bloodied nose mutters gruffly that he might have to take legal action, and his loving wife, a handsome chesty woman, says: "It was about time someone shut you up."

A young nun glides silently through the crowded room, her scapular hanging rakishly off her shoulders, working her rosary beads between her fingers in such a way as to make me think of a woman fingering her clitoris. She exudes a ripe aroma. Her presence brings a sense of decorum to the room, and a sense of scandal. A chunky gent in a bright plaid sports jacket and grass-stained white trousers approaches her respectfully and asks: "Is life for real, mother, or only a clever illusion?" "Doubt, my son," she replies, raising one hand in a kind of blessing, "is the beginning of faith." "And the end of faith," I say. The look she gives me is one of reprobation. And of desire.

There's someone hanging on my elbow. It's the bony woman with the prominent proboscis. She whispers loudly in my ear, spraying saliva into it, that she has a cash buyer, and she hands me a small handful of bills. A joke, not remotely close to my asking price, but when I reject the offer by tossing the money disdainfully over my shoulder, the lady realtor and I are set upon by a couple of thugs, demanding the key to the safe. The tough they work for, arms folded over his belly near the door, is grinning malevolently around the unlit cigar he's chewing on like he knows I'm a fraud and will soon pay for it. A loathsome lot, but no one has a divine right to the world's money, else I'd be without a career.

I have to somehow use the handing over of the keys as a means to escape my captors, but they grab my thumbs and bend them back to my wrists, causing me to squeak with pain, and snatch the key ring out of my hands. I am still trying to find a plausible excuse for why none of the keys fit the lock—when, amazingly, one *does* fit, and the safe is opened! It's packed with money, and the penthouse deed is in there as well! The thugs and their boss, hruffing throatily, treat themselves to lavish tips, press a few bills on the realtor, and let both of us go. The penthouse deed and that shocking pile of loose cash are technically mine, of course, and, as the generous ex-owner, I'd like to stay long enough to get my hands on some of it, but it's hard to pick pockets with swollen thumbs; my luck may be running out up here.

The party crowd seems to regard me as the butt of some joke, so, winking back at them as though to imply that I'm in on the gag and may indeed have instituted it, I move calmly but quickly out to the elevator in the entrance hall. The door's conveniently agape. I step inside and punch the ground floor button, regretting only that I failed to pocket some of those loose bills when the realtor handed them to me. The door closes, and there is a sudden drop that momentarily leaves me afloat, then brings me to my knees when it stops with a jolt, but when the door opens again, I'm still in the penthouse entranceway. I crawl out and hear the elevator descending. This is alarming, I tell myself, getting to my feet, but also in some manner explicable. I seem to know things, accept them, and not know or accept them at the same time.

The bosomy wife of the mustachioed fellow belted by the bartender, is standing sentinel-like outside the elevator door in a state of self-righteous fury. "This is your home," she declares, "and it has been unfairly taken away from you. We cannot let such evil prevail." I ask her, massaging my bruised thumbs, if she has the least notion of what evil truly is, and she replies coolly, as something else is taken away, that it is whatever disturbs the way things are. "No, not a divine order," I say, when he sarcastically suggests that as my underlying belief. "More like the social glue that keeps everything from falling apart." He grunts, shuddering, and it feels like something almost physical has happened between us. I flick a half smile in his direction to reassure him and to acknowledge our mutual understanding, though I'm not confident of it. He's a weak man, an opportunist, perhaps acting in collusion with the despicable subhuman who ostensibly just bought his home, though more likely he's the ruffian's prey, just as he was preyed upon by the conniving woman. A cynical aristocrat softened by wealth, easily manipulated, believing only in life's ultimate meaninglessness, and the freedom that gives him. But he has virtues. He dealt forcefully nough with the brainless bartender who struck my husband, and, though he first ran away from the hoodlums who have taken possession of his home, he has now returned, so it seems, to face them again. And he is not bad looking. I find myself falling in love with him, though love is probably not the word. Rather, a sense of rightness and inevitability about our eventual partnership.

"The theft of your home is wickedness enough, but there has also been a murder," I inform him, hiding the news under the noisy chatter all around us, "or perhaps more properly, an execution. One of the musicians you hired heaved an old blind man over your terrace railing, unaware that I was watching. When he learned I'd witnessed the murder, he was struck with fear, needless to say, and, had we been out back, he might have tried desperately to duplicate his feat with me as his victim; but, inside, among others, he quietly offered me what he amateurishly called 'hush money.' I of course rejected it, curious to see what he'd do next." As I'd hoped, the penthouse's former owner smiles faintly in response to this news and waits, as I waited, for what more is to be revealed. Perhaps he is also falling in love. "Your musician broke down and related a horrifying story of vicious beatings and cruel intimidations by the old composer and his colleagues. He said they had ruined his life. He was weeping pitiably. I was touched." In reality, the musician's egoistic sniveling disgusted me, though I knew he needed someone like me, and his servile participation would make much else possible. And now perhaps I will have this powerful man's alliance as well. I feel something accumulating in me, not unlike power.

The guests here tonight are mostly a loud and frivolous lot, heavy drinkers not thinkers, but there must be some who are self-lessly devoted to the preservation of our social fabric, a precious tapestry woven long before we were born, and ever under threat of being ripped asunder. We must identify those fellow patri-ots, and draw them, arousing their own best instincts, toward us. This is what I feel in the depths of my being, as I explain to the true owner now. In the main reception room, there is a huge work of art, a photographic collage taking up a whole wall. It is a giant black-and-white portrait of a great wartime leader, made up of thousands of smaller monochromes, as though to suggest that his leadership represents something larger than any one person, including himself, merely a container of sorts. That image of the ultimate unity of disparate elements must guide us. And the amazing thing is that the heroic leader, though one has to step back further than the room allows to see the collage with perfect clarity, looks a lot like the former owner of this penthouse, the man I am now facing.

"The contrabassist is a handsome man, tall and bony with silky hair down to his elbows, but, as he himself admits, he is, like most sedentary persons, a physical weakling. So, I was frankly amazed when he tossed that heavyset old boy over the terrace railing like a feather pillow. He confessed to me that the man seemed to grow lighter as he lifted him, almost as though someone were helping him, which I took to be a sign of the ennobling strength of righteous action kicking in. The discredited old composer was an obstacle to progress and other committed persons like ourselves must be found to augment our ranks. In short, I said to the bass player as I say to you now: we must organize. I am gratified that you seem prepared to be an active participant." The ex-owner's complaisant shrug tells me that, since being stripped of his possessions, his options have narrowed, but he clearly has no appetite for the hard work of resistance. No matter. He can represent our cause as its icon, a victim of incivility, and we will do the rest. And perhaps he's lonely for a meaningful connection. "We'll have to recruit a few foot soldiers as well, as I'm sure you'll understand. They may not be sophisticated persons, but they are required for the tasks we face, and are fortunately expendable."

Of course, my husband opposed my engagement in this matter, as he opposes every action that I take, whining that

I always get it all wrong. He's a wine snob, and all night he has been belaboring the other guests with tedious disquisitions on varietals and vintages, quoting his dubious authorities, bullying the young bartender at every opportunity, finally getting his nose deservedly hammered. His wine knowledge was once part of his charm; now, it merely exhibits his abusive arrogance. When the penthouse thieves are eventually dispatched, he'll have to go, too. He is not well, his heart is fragile, he faces inevitable catastrophic illness; we'll be doing him a favor, really.

With the bassist, we already have the services of the most reliable of the several professionals on duty here tonight, possibly excepting the chief cook. The bartender, though cute, is, alas, an ill-tempered devotee of that which he serves, the caterer has telltale needle tracks up both her arms, the saxophonist is rude and, like my husband, is all too full of himself, and the crazed pianist never actually plays anything recognizable, just keeps his fingers moving fast and his body bouncing, as though that's all that popular music *is*: overwrought gesture. A fake; he can't be trusted, none of them can. But we will need someone to do the heavy lifting, and the chief cook, however stupid—a trait that may in the end prove to be an asset—appears to have the requisite strength. And he cooks well, if he cooks at all. He's continuously pulling amazing things, hot and ready to eat, out of the oven, though I've not yet seen him put anything *in*. A minor quibble. As a disgruntled foreigner, he probably hates everybody up here, and won't object to anything that the owner deems must be done to protect the community.

So it is that, with the handsome penthouse owner at my side, we are just striding toward the reception room, full of noble ambitions, when the elevator doors spring open, and we are engulfed by an explosive flood of loud narcissistic partygoers. One of them, shouting that he can't wait and, clutching the stained crotch of his shabby suit trousers, knocks me rudely to the floor, before smashing his way into a nearby restroom, bursting in on me while still unzipping his fly: *"You gonna be much longer, lady? I gotta GO!"*

"Come ahead," I sigh, wiping myself and flushing. "I'm done." I pull up my panties, feeling oddly like there's something in them. I tug them back down for a quick look: no, they're clean. But something . . . The man shoves me urgently out of his way, and I stumble, thighs bound by elastic, to the wash basin, where I'm confronted by a mirrored vision of my sorry plight. I accept the image with a shrug, pull my underwear up again. Say la vee, as the expression goes. While there, I check my lipstick, the gentleman splashing away beside me, groaning and cursing softly, poor man (is that blood?); then I straighten my skirt, spray on more perfume, pick up my purse and wineglass, and slip out, avoiding the bossy lady posted, arms folded indignantly, just outside the restroom door.

It's very crowded now, more people really than the penthouse can hold, but the elevator door slides open again, and yet

more rambunctious guests come squeezing in, the walls seeming almost to back away, as if the apartment were stretching to
make room for everybody. An illusion, of course; my life is full of
them. Someone takes a grip on my bottom, but I don't even try to
see who it is, I just sip my wine and think about the hand while
it's still oh so briefly there. I've put on years and weight, and no
one does that much anymore. It's sort of what parties are for.
Human contact. The rare blind pleasure of it. I never miss one, if
I can help it, knowing I'll be disappointed, but, as is my nature,
remaining ever hopeful, though I don't know for what.

In the front room, where the other bodies are pushing me,
obliging me to go where they go, I spot the bearded man in the
crumpled fedora I rode up here with on the elevator, now conversing earnestly with a neatly dressed lady with graying hair. He
seems to be admonishing her. That gentleman had nice things
to say to me that I'd so much love to hear again. I didn't exactly
understand them the first time, but

I feel smarter now, as though whatever was in my panties
might have perked up my tired old brain, as far apart from each
other as they are, if that makes sense, so I try to work my way
through the crowd toward him.

Alas, there are too many rowdy people in the way, my poor
clumsy body finally getting bumped into a room I was in before,
where that young man with the funny pigtails is still playing the
grand piano. Sort of playing it. He seems in a rage about something and is mostly just making noise by banging his fists on the

keys, as if punishing them for not doing what he wants them to do. I ask him in a hopefully friendly manner what the make of the piano is, it doesn't seem to have a nameplate, but he just keeps hitting it. Probably it's too cheap a thing to name, I've just made a fool of myself again.

The other two musicians pay no attention to him, or to each other either. The double bassist is mumbling to himself, eyes closed under his curtain of hair, while he plucks the strings, though it doesn't sound exactly *like* plucking, and the overweight saxophone player, who was making such a dreadful racket blowing on his instrument last time, is quiet now, a puzzled expression on his broad moony face. He is holding lightbulbs in his hands that have been removed from the room's lamps, but that, amazingly, are still brightly lit. He throws them at the floor and stamps on them, but they keep right on glowing. Trick bulbs probably. People are watching him with amusement, but he is not amused.

It's crowded here in the den, too, and hard to hear the musicians or anything else. When a trim lady wearing librarian-style wire-rims leans close to my ear and asks me something indistinct about the lights on the floors below, I can only smile and apologize. Then, seeing the catering woman passing through with her silver tray held aloft, I ask the bespectacled lady if she has tasted the extraordinary appetizers. I cannot hear her reply; perhaps she could not hear my question. I accept a roasted oyster on a skewer and, with a friendly smile, offer it to her, but she only sniffs petulantly and marches away. Too bad. Yum. It's so delicious, it must be fattening.

"This party reminds me of the old high school bio-lab experiments," rumbles a bald skinny man with a jutting bewhiskered chin, squinting through cracked bifocals. I have no idea what he means. We must have attended different high schools. When a husky young woman in bluejeans adds, "Right, with booze as the chemical trail," I'm utterly lost. I know what booze is, but science was always my worst subject. I never knew what to say when called on by the teacher. Once, in a shameful moment, I even soiled my panties in the chemistry lab out of sheer terror with the teacher staring straight at me. Mortification was what science was mostly about for me.

Two boys wearing wide-brimmed cowboy hats chase a squealing girl through the crowd, in one door and out another. Some kind of party game probably, they are all three laughing crazily, the boys barking like dogs, the girl screaming something in a foreign language like something has gotten into *her* panties. There was a day when I might have joined in the fun, but now even *thinking* about running gives me palpitations. It's all about that, isn't it? Knowing your limits. Then doing what you can with what you've been given. I often say the wrong thing and do the wrong thing, but one thing I've been given is that, underneath it all, I am a nice person and I like other people who are also nice.

The crowd's on the move again and I move along with them into the next room, having little choice. When I was in this room a little while ago, I saw a gentleman who seemed to be the host of this party, a nice man who was patient with fat dummies like me, though I understand he may have sold his apartment tonight to someone who is not so nice. I'm not sure how I understand that, but the how's not important, only the understanding is, and maybe that's not important either. The nice man was graciously asking everybody how they learned about the party, but I had forgotten, if I ever knew, so I told him instead that I simply adored the fantastic musicians. He winced like he was suffering sudden gas pains and pushed away to the next room. Oh dear. All I want really, having tiny little hopes but no expectations, is the opportunity to meet nice people, and, even if this wonderful apartment is no longer his, I would be happy to be of service to him in any way he wants.

The not-so-nice man with the nose ring who is said to be the new owner comes over now with two rough-looking fellows and slaps my behind, rather too hard, shouting at me that I have a grand patootie. I don't know what a patootie is, but I can guess. "Are you a nice person?" I ask him. He makes a sour face and moves on, his friends following, toward a little cluster of young girls with smaller patooties. "Don't go away, I *love* to be spanked," I call after him, even though there's nothing I like less; I'm only sorry if I hurt his feelings. But he's gone, without looking back, and his friends, too. I'm so clumsy, and now it's say la vee all over again. The young girls are tittering (laughing at me?) with their hands over their mouths as though afraid they might have bad breath.

When the young nun who rode up with me on the elevator comes past, I curtsey, hoping it's all right to do that. It seems to be. She smiles warmly at me, which is the nicest response I've had all night, and I wonder if I wouldn't be happier in her religion than whatever I'm in now. She doesn't smell as nice as she looks, though it's an honest human smell. And perhaps she's not as young as I first thought, but even her wrinkles are beautiful.

"When that nun passed by," a silver-haired gentleman, his voice quavery and his eyes rolled back, declares, "I felt close to the Lord!"

"Oh yes," I say, leaning in. "Me too!"

"Maybe, but not so close as *me*," says one of those boys in cowboy hats who were just running through here. "She squeezed my dick when she blowed by, and look what she *done* to it!" I gasp and lean away. "I been goddamn *blessed*, man!"

My pal's dong is hanging outside his pants, puffed up big as a fencepost and oozing at the tip—and it's *green*! Even his meatballs are green! *Paintbox* green! "Holy shit, man! The nun did that—?"

"Yeah, and I'm so fuckin' fried, all I could do was laugh!"

"It *is* pretty funny," I say, feeling uneasy about the dude's monster green boner and this big-bucks mass-up he's dragged me to. "Sort of goes with your hot orange tee." This is not my scene at all. Sex-mad nuns, yes; nuns with green thumbs, no. And it doesn't feel generally all that healthy up here. Fucking axe up there somewhere, ready to fall. I'd drop a blast to the followers, warning them about what's going down here, but my frigging phone's not working. Bad vibes in the high-altitude air maybe. "Now, why don't you put that silly banana back in its sack, pal, and let it ripen?"

"Nah, it's too itchy. Anyhow, it don't seem to fit in my pants no more."

"Too stiff?"

"Don't know. Too something."

This crazy dude and I first met online. Didn't take long to figure out that we hate the same kind of people, have the same cool fuck-you style, collect freedom weapons bigtime, groove on splatter flicks and old black-and-white westerns, hot chicken wings and cold beer, and prefer pros who know how to suck cock properly over sloppy schoolyard brats. He learned I always wear sweaty wide-brimmed Stets, so he stole a used one for himself, no doubt off of some suddenly dead man's head. Trouble is, it's a size or two too big, but he says he digs the stupid look, makes people think he's only kidding while he's wasting them. I'm maybe more hardcore in how I relate to the sicko world, he mostly just digs the violence. Since for me, life amounts to shit and everybody is better off dead, our notions come to much the same thing in the end. Better to be dead before you know what's happening. A bullet in the brain is a happy ending.

The day we first got together in person, he introduced me to a coke dealer he knows. He was already wearing his comical Stet down around his ears, and I laughed when I saw it, said it was cool. The dealer was just closing a sale with some client, and the cash on display hit my pal-to-be like a spark hits a powder keg. He grabbed the bills and set them aflame with a cigarette lighter, and when the guy tried to grab the money back, my pal reached in his waistband, pulled out a revolver, and blew him away. Which left me no choice but to take out the dealer's mark so as to leave no witnesses. We've been tight ever since. Ants and bees don't care who dies or when, why should we?

So, I was easy pickings for his invite to this fancyass dump tonight, which he says some bird tipped him to. Not sure why he digs it up here. Nobody's wearing a ten-gee or looking for action, stupid drunks mostly, blowing sickly sweet party smoke and sucking up the freebies. Maybe my pal wants to get close to all the torchable money. Me, I don't trust anything about this fatcat scene, would cut out in a minute.

I sure as hell don't trust the bosomy battleship bearing down on us now. She has the strongarm moves of a fucking homeroom monitor. A boss lady. There's an uptight shithead with her who my pal says is, or was, the owner of this glitzy pad, plus a tall skinny faggot with long stringy hair down to his butt, but the two look easy enough to take down, even if my pal is finally too freaked out to lend a hand. Maybe the boss lady saw us roughing up that damned foreign cunt for refusing a perfectly reasonable ask, two for the price of one, and it pissed her off. Whatever, I feel an urge to waste the officious twat. Don't know where the urge comes from (where does *any* urge come from?), but—*wait!* where the fuck are my *tools?* I slap my empty pockets—my *cannons* are gone! Backpack with the spare ammo, too! I yelp to the boss lady about the vanished hardware, and she says, no problem, you won't need them. But it *is* a problem, goddamn it! Losing them makes me feel like I've dropped my flipping pants in the middle of rush-hour traffic! When I tell her that, she only laughs, the bitch.

She points out a smug sleazebag with white handlebars, passing by on his way to the house bar, and says she wants us to help her throw that bum off the roof terrace. He's a rapist billionaire, she says, who uses his money to buy hitmen to blow away the competition and to knock off any women he's used up. Don't know if that's true or not, but we both hate big-bucks assholes, so it sounds like a cool thing to do. But, first, I have to get my bangsticks back. "They cost me a shitpotfulla money I don't have," I say, unloosing a wad of chaw, but she shrugs off my gut-wrenching panic. It's harder to shrug off my pal's green dick, and she doesn't. She asks him if it hurts, and my pal says it doesn't, but the itch is driving him out of his fucking mind! The boss lady says she has a lotion in her raincoat pocket that might help; if it's still there, she'll pass it on to him next time she sees him. She has nothing that fixes my clenched gut.

She asks my pal how it happened, and when she hears about the nun squeezing it green, she says she has hated nuns ever since three of them abused her daisy-chainwise in a locked chapel, when she was just a little girl. They told her it would be fun, and it wasn't. "Maybe," she says, "the nun will join the rapist on his farewell flight," and she winks. A tougher cunt than I thought. My pal waggles his arms, suggesting he's imagining those two dumb motherfuckers flapping their arms desperately while dropping through naked space—*flap! flap! flap!*—and that *is* pretty funny. My mind, though, is mainly on that daisy chain, wondering exactly what part this tough lady played in it as a kid. Were the nuns stripped to their skinny or still in their stinking woollies? I see them on all fours on the altar, locked in place by wrist and ankle cuffs, white butts high, but I'm not thinking about fucking those butts, only of whipping them or watching them being whipped. Nuns force people to live the lie that life is good; they deserve whatever happens to them. Punishment of bad girls is, for me, a massive turn-on, all the more so when it's holier-than-thou types getting their big pale asses lashed. Hard enough to bleed. Red on white: lovely.

The boss lady compliments my pal on his cowboy hat, tee shirt, and the black string tie, knotted around his naked neck, and says that that combination might work as the new movement's official uniform. We just stare at her. The only movements we take seriously are bowel movements, but we don't tell her that, what good would it do? To tell the truth, we're not hot on the idea of other cocksuckers wearing our trademark duds. I don't trust her as far as I could throw her, but she's setting us up to a bit of much-needed action, best to collect on that first. The whore tosses her head as a way of ordering us to follow her, the pushy cunt, and they leave together, that woman, the man she came in with, and those two troublemakers. On the way out the door, the woman glances back over her shoulder, appraising me. I was the one who warned her about the violent nature of those young men, and now I regret that, seeing how chummy they've become, and maybe always were. I should know better.

The woman is with a good-looking man I have been assuming is the owner of this penthouse apartment, though maybe he's been cheated out of it, and is now only the *former* owner. Not sure about that, but it makes a more coherent story; meaning, it's more likely to be true. Narrative truth: the only sort one can trust in the end. In the course of his interrogation as to how we found the party (we didn't, the party found us), I remarked in passing on the darkness of all the floors below this one. He was surprised and, at the time, seemed intrigued, but I regret that, too. I didn't know then that he was the penthouse owner and host of this party and would partner with that woman and those horrible boys. There's something sinister happening, just under the surface, or maybe right in plain sight, and they seem to be part of it. Unscrupulous rich man, vampish woman with ambition—the collusion of such archetypes provides the plots of many of my best-loved stories. So, keep your eyes open and your mouth shut. Write. Then leave it on the page, a principle I used to live by and should still.

I came here with a gentleman whom I've known for years, a lawyer friend of my deceased husband. We were planning on a

quiet supper in a nearby restaurant, but he was suddenly fasci-
nated by the lights at the top of this otherwise darkened building,
and insisted we go see what's going on. "I hear party music," he
shouted, already moving toward the open gate. When I remarked
on all the unlit floors, he only laughed his big ebullient laugh.
"You're a writer!" he roared. "You make things up! Come on!" His
callow insensitivity frightened me. I've needed someone with
whom to share my thoughts tonight, but he is probably not the one.

We were separated on arrival by a slow-moving mass of chat-
tering guests, and, though we haven't had a moment together
since, I have heard him, even when he's in another room: he
`doesn't talk, he *bellows*. I'd leave immediately on my own, but
I've seen people trying that and the elevator doesn't seem to be
functioning properly. There were no locks on the street-level
doors, none up here either. Is that a metaphor for something? Or
is it more ominous than that? Is this building a trap?

I've spoken with others about my apprehensions, but so far
there has been no helpful response. Rarely even an acknowledge-
ment of the facts, which they dismiss as mere fiction, seeming to
recognize me and what I famously do. It's true, I sometimes do
find myself adrift in plots mostly of my own invention, almost
believing in the factuality of them, but I think of such missteps
as part of my vocation. At the same time, after all, even during
the missteps, I've been gifted with intuitive leaps of the sort that
would have solved many real crimes, so-called, and that usually
do solve those I've made up.

If this were one of my stories, I'd probably imagine this penthouse as the melancholic setting for the universal metaphor, the experience of nothingness, afloat in or on darkness. A romantic image, to be sure; melancholy *is* romantic. My heroines have often endured just such clichés, my readers as well, but I am a romancer and I need familiar old plots, however trite, to help me think, find the words. There are not many of them—usable words, I mean—and all too easily they slip from memory's feeble grasp. Story makes them less slippery.

In one of my more anthologized stories, two people meet at a party much like this one, except that it is ostensibly a wake for a very old person, so not so noisy. They both feel a romantic attachment growing between them, but because they are strangers at a wake, they are unable to express their true feelings. The dialogue presented me with the challenge of saying everything and nothing at the same time, but without the benefit of suggestive innuendo, inappropriate at a wake. At the end of the frustrating night, they part and never see each other again. Years later, the woman is trying to remember what those "true feelings" were, and she realizes that, with the passing years, the mystery at attraction's core has only deepened, the language for the crisis more inaccessible than ever. In effect, it is a still unrealized writing task, and has become the subliminal theme of my current story-in-progress.

When I told the bearded man in the soft beat-up headpiece that I was trying to finish a new story—not this one, of course, though now I'm beginning to see how it might be developed—he reminded me pedantically that the most interesting stories are the unfinished ones. He himself seemed unfinished in some odd way; I found it difficult to see both his eyes as belonging to the same face. "Leave it open," he scolded. "Unresolved."

"I always do," I answered, "but the failure to finish a story element needs its own raison-d'être, something that is itself an integral piece of the plot."

"No," he insisted stubbornly, "it does not. If you think so, the truth will always elude you."

"Maybe," I snapped back, growing tired of this old man, whom I later learned is an unknown experimental taleteller of some dubious sort, "but, as I'm unable to find a satisfactory definition of 'truth,' I have to rely upon narrative cohesion for what truth remains."

He tipped his battered fedora sadly, adding melancholy to melancholy, and turned away.

I take a note, wondering if subliminality itself might be, in effect, the key to resolving that quandary so long weighing on me, providing thereby a satisfying ending to my story, while at the same time opening a passage into the new one. I write a large "YES!" beside my note, and pocket the notebook, a gesture which has always reassured me in moments of self-doubt. It is that gesture of slipping my notebook into a pocket that most convinces me that, however ephemeral my fame as a novelist might be, my notebook—not really "mine" any longer—will, preserved and protected by librarians, grammarians, and other devotees of the Word, live on for all written time. Which is not all that long a time perhaps, but in the absence of a human forever, it's the best there is.

An elderly thin man with a very sad face, shoveled into the room through the door at my elbow by the insistent flow of the crowd, brings yet more melancholy into play. He seems beyond cheer; perhaps—pitiably—not all there. I ask him, having to shout, if he is enjoying the party, and, leaning heavily on his cane, he gives me a lost vacant look that is truly heart-breaking in its emptiness. He's like a walking metaphor for sadness. It takes an effort not to be terrorized by the human reality. We spend our lives building memories, or tell ourselves that's what we're doing, and senility, when it arrives, as it must, if one lives long enough, wipes everything out. We are not emanations of a thinking God—this is the thought that comes to me, and I get my notebook out again to jot a note—but of a digesting God. The sorrowful ancient seems incapable of speech, but then he does speak, as he gets pushed along: "This party is going to end badly," he says into the clamor, or something like that. Perhaps he has said nothing, only groaned, but that is his groan's essence, and I believe him.

A lurking question: what is the meaning of all the floors below this one being dark? The sort of question I ask all too often in my restless search for the truth, my notebooks are full of them. The bushily bearded man reminded me not to look for meaning where there is none—I know that, though I sometimes forget—so, maybe I don't mean "meaning." Something more like the compelling exigencies of the storyline. Ultimately, that storyline is almost always, for me, a love story, though, in this case, one with a tragic heroine, for whom gratification comes at a terrible price. Again, in my writing anyway, a frequent commonplace, but one experienced, with each new project, as most uncommon, completely new. That's the miracle of story-telling. The writer asserts. Hopefully.

It's at this moment that, like a gift to the faltering narrator, the alleged new owner makes his entrance. The perfect heavy, with dark overhanging brows, a big belly, a face scarred with acne, a natural scowl, a fat half-eaten cigar, a cynical smile. He tops it all off with a gold nose ring, as though he were married to his nose. He glances around the room, no doubt looking for randy young women, eager for a slightly dangerous one-night fling, like those giggling girls over there. If this were my story, I might make him the misunderstood hero, a man who accepts life's indignities with a dark mysterious smile. In my story, he gazes tenderly upon the heroine, wishing he were other than what he appears to be. In reality, he ignores me altogether, approaching instead a group of his party guests, including my deceased husband's lawyer friend, who signals to me to join them. The cynical cigar-eater says something that makes everyone bray with laughter, and the cigar-eater laughs, too, snorting loudly, but not so loudly as my lawyer friend.

I turn away from their mock-hilarity and step through a door I feel certain I've walked through before, but into a room I haven't yet visited, a games room of sorts. The party music is louder in here, but the source is as mysterious as ever. People are playing charades and strip poker, tossing ping pong balls in some kind of mindless drinking game, shooting pool with bent cues. Pinning the tail on the donkey becomes sticking paper eyes on bare bottoms. A lot of squealing and obnoxious laughter, heavy pall of evil smoke. I hate this party, feel abused by it. I want to go home!

While searching resolutely for an exit, I pass a window onto the lighted roof terrace and become a witness to what appears to be, in the shadows, a cold-blooded murder: those two violent boys I warned that business woman about are throwing her old white-mustachioed husband, kicking and flailing, over the garden railing! My scream is lost in the room's drunken racket. There's a door nearby that leads to the terrace, but I'm too frightened to use it, though the poor woman who has just been widowed is out there somewhere, and may need help. When someone touches me, she shrieks in terror and strikes out at me.

"Easy, easy, my dear! Ow! Ha ha! It's only your old lawyer friend!"

"Oh! I'm so sorry!" She falls against me, moaning softly, then abruptly pushes me away. "Did you *see* that?" she cries. "We must call the *police*! That lady's husband—!"

"Yes, of course," I say cheerfully, guiding her out of the crowded games room into the mass-up in the next. Police? She's a writer and needs constant reassurance that the world is not as crazy as she is. "But, as you know, this apartment is bless-edly free of landlines, and mobiles don't seem to work up here." I laugh, hoping to distract her from whatever nonsense is on her little mind, worried only that it might be infecting my own. "It's what makes everything so *pleasant!*"

"But it was *murder!* I *saw* it! Those boys in cowboy hats—!"

"Okay, sure, in that case, I'll see what I can do," I say, laughing again, and smooth my thinning hair down. On the pretense of chasing down her nonsensical concerns, I step away from the poor woman and the stifling pack-up inside, and out onto the roof terrace. Good lord! I've been through these paranoid delusions and bouts of hysteria many times, but they never cease to astonish me. Murder! Cowboy hats! What next? Her husband, on his deathbed, warned me that she can be a danger to herself, and begged me to watch over her. I have tried to be faithful to his plea, though it has been a constant trial.

There are scores of people out here, too, but nothing like the congestion inside. As I expected, there's nothing amiss: the buxom wife of the white-haired gentleman in question—the writer's alleged "murder victim"—is strolling through the roof-top garden in the twilight with the former penthouse owner in a casual manner that suggests that neither of them has beheld any untoward events. Maybe they're involved in an affair of their own, their relaxed demeanor suggests a certain mature intimacy, but it's not something that interests me, unless one of them needs a divorce lawyer. My friend's wife lives in a reality of her own invention, like too many lady novelists. She should probably give up the writing, it's not good for her mental health—it's not good for anyone's, to tell the truth, particularly for persons predisposed to lunacy—but I won't be the one to tell her that. There's a limit to what one can do as a friend. Tomorrow I'll look into ways she can be institutionally cared for. Just in case.

My relationship with her and her husband began with a legal evaluation of his investments (it required moving some assets out of the country, something I could discreetly arrange), but it soon evolved into a personal friendship, which in turn led to my quiet attempts to provide him occasional sanctuary from his wife's peculiar excesses. We held light-hearted business lunches in wine bars, enjoyed a few stag night poker parties, disguised as investment opportunities, and when a former nun broke her vows—though not that of chastity—to become a stripper, I organized an evening "tax consultation," so that I could take him to her opening coming-out show. To this day, she still goes onstage in her entire religious costume, because, comically enough, she apparently thinks of herself as a stripper for the Lord. Divesting herself of her complicated habit makes for a long show, with hairshirts and sackcloth and other punishing underwear along the way, but the wait is worth it, especially when she invites you to lick the little trickles of thorn-pricked blood, which she calls, without a trace of irony, "taking communion." My appreciative friend took communion several times, and announced afterwards that he did indeed feel spiritually uplifted. Maybe she's the one who's here tonight, maybe not; they all look the same to me in their costumes. Probably taste differently, though. Maybe there's even a cult of stripper nuns. Many ways to serve the Divinity.

The sun is going down. Days are a few minutes longer up here, high above the street. Soon enough, it will be dark, though the terrace is electrically well-lit, in accordance with the lawful regulations. The alcoholic realtor with the big nose staggers past now with another glass of colored gin in her hand, muttering insensibly to herself, a warped grin on her face. No doubt feeling flush, if in her inebriation she can feel anything at all. This penthouse is a charming piece of property and a short while ago she offered it to me at terms that were extremely attractive, but under conditions that seemed, starting with the current owner's demand for immediate cash only, legally dubious at best. Presumably, the former owner was on the run, though in fact he's still here.

Eventually, a new client of mine—new tonight—picked it up for a song, and we have found the entire process a bit outside customary business practices, but more or less aboveboard. He now hopes to find a new buyer here tonight and turn a quick profit. He asked me to make an offer, but I declined on grounds of conflict of interest, eliciting a sarcastic grin. I remain doubtful of the entire enterprise in truth, my client seeming to be one who lives at the margins of the law, but I say nothing that might interfere with an eventual commission. Were I here alone, I'd stay to see what amusement or business might arise, but it's past the good lady's bedtime. I give the man my card, apologizing for the early departure, and remind him to call me at home, if he needs me. There is perhaps time to stop at a restaurant on our way home, that having been our original plan—the appetizers have been sensational, but they've done nothing to curb the appetite—but, unless the novelist requests it, I'd prefer to see her home and dine alone.

I find her in the penthouse library, seated on an antique chaise lounge, notepad on her knee, assiduously composing another unreadable best-seller. Books line the walls like musty remnants of a past long and gratefully dead. No crowds in here, though there's a sign announcing a gathering of the reading club later on, focused on a book from the library: "Transcendentalism and *Group Sex.*" "Come," I say gently, sobered by the spare surroundings, and take her hand. "I do understand your concerns. We're leaving." She reminds me that the elevator isn't working, and I laugh, tell her that of course it's working, and pull her out of the library past the grinning nun toward the open elevator door in the entrance hall.

She clings to me, afraid to let go, but also afraid to enter the elevator. "It won't go down!" she insists. "It *will*," I yell, laughing, and drag her in with me. But she's right. I punch the down button, the elevator drops, stops hard enough to throw us to our knees, and when the door opens, we're still in the entrance hall, with three giggling girls trying to enter. "It's not working!" I shout, crawling out, but they push me aside and eagerly pile in. *Wait! My friend's wife has been left behind!* I bang my fists frantically on the elevator door. The elevator makes grinding noises like it's digesting something, and then the doors open and the three young things, their pleated skirts around their waists, tumble out in a tearful daze, tittering nervously, the lady novelist crawling out behind them. I don't know what's happening, except that I'm feeling decidedly unlawyerly.

A heavyset horsey woman, entering from the terrace garden in bluejeans, approaches us. "I think I know you," she says to the woman I'm with, still on her knees, and tears a page from her notebook. "Can I have your autograph? I'm a huge fan of all your books!"

"*What—!?*" my friend shrieks, shrinking away.

"Enough of this idiocy! We'll *walk* down!" I yell angrily and, grabbing the lady's hand, haul her to her feet and stumble past the autograph seeker to the nearest EXIT sign. Jocular whoops are still pouring out of me like canned laughter in a sitcom, but in truth I'm scared shitless! She holds back—"I wouldn't . . . " she cries—but his grip is too tight and they disappear through the exit door, pages from her notebook flying, which, even as she falls, she tries to snatch back (it must be the writer in her),

her scream, his roar of dismay providing the show's fade-away background music. No one else notices this, as far as I can tell. In fact, I can't say for sure, as the door slowly closes, that I've seen what I've just seen. The twitchy old preacher, who's been badgering me with his holy asininities, says they've found the Lord, which, as a punchline, can mean only one thing. I'm thinking of the ending of that writer's best-seller about the farm girl who, fed up with milking cows and beheading chickens, storms out of the farmhouse one day, banging the screen door behind her, and is never seen again, a story that is said to haunt the author to this day. Of course, I haven't exactly *read* it, more like I've read *about* it—the critics treat it like it's the cat's meow, even though it doesn't even have a proper fucking ending—but that's the gist, as I understand it.

I *do*, however, know all about banging screen doors, they echo through my life like blattery thunderclaps. My novel-in-progress is also set on a farm, not a fake farm made up by a citified twit, but the real one I grew up on with farting cows and lukewarm milk straight from the udder and shit-filled chicken coops that had to be swept, plus a mentally defective beekeeper for a father, abusive brothers, and an unloving mother who blithely took off with some rough beardy guy soon after I was born—the real McCoy, not just made-up words strung together like fucking tree lights. Write about what you know, as they preach at you in the workshops; or so they tell me, never having been accepted into one, but, in any event, I have done so. And my story, like the romancer's—she *has* to *love* it—also has to do with an oppressed young heroine, mired in chicken shit and cow dung, breaking loose. Banging the goddamn screen door on the way out, why not? *Whap!*

When I first caught sight of the famous novelist, I thought it was going to be my lucky day. I've read every interview she's ever given, a sharp and testy voice, but one that sympathizes with the underdog, and I was sure she'd agree to read the manuscript of my first novel, already nearly twelve pages long, and would give it her blessing, maybe even a blurb when I get around to needing one. As usual, though, it looks like I'm fucked again. It's not even clear, with the elevator busted, how I'll make it back down to the street.

I don't get many calls for interviews, in fact I get none, but I have often interviewed myself. Sometimes I'm a rich and famous writer, the first woman to use "fuck" five times on the same page; at other times I'm a woefully underrated rebel, hated and dismissed for the same word that in another scenario has made me famous. The interviewer is smart and always gets right to the meat. She wants to know what I think about death, and I tell her I'm disappointed by it, but I'm not fighting it, I've got too much else on my plate. When she asks me about love, I say it's a game rich people play. Can be fun, but mostly it's fatal. The interviewer tells me I know nothing about true love, but what does she know, the fatassed bitch? Has she dropped a kid like I have with no husband in sight and then had the dumb kid croak on her, just because she's got nothing to give it to eat but its own shit? True love! Come on, give me a break, I tell myself.

My readers naturally want to know more about the abusive brothers. I could whip up a tale about how they threw me down in the filthy chicken coop and raped me in front of all the noisy cluckers. That's not exactly how it was, but porn sells, so probably the heroine gets a couple of brotherly dicks up her ass in the stinking chicken coop. What really happened was that, when I bared my butt for them, the bastards kicked it. I called them faggots, and they kicked it again. Harder. So, yes, they were abusive. Is that the true story? Maybe. What does it matter if I fudge on the details? It's called being creative, and in writing circles, that's a big fucking deal. Not that I've made it into those circles. I've sent a thousand applications off to writing schools, but so far no takers. Sure, I've refused to pay their idiot fees and said some nasty things about them, but even when I've given in to the elitist twerps, filled out the fucking forms and sent in the rip-off fees, it was time and money wasted. The truth is, as I told the interviewer, they're afraid of me.

A pair of cowboys in wide-brimmed Stets, one in a glowing orange tee shirt, the other in a leather vest of unknown vintage and a dirty white undershirt, come on to me in the front hall, both looking wild and dangerous. I get ready to kick them in the balls and yell for help, if I have to, but they only want to talk. Maybe they have an offer to make. They ask me what I do for a living, and I tell them I'm a writer, though the world doesn't know that yet. "Right now, I'm in serious need of a plot change that can get me off the farm and into a fancy dump like this one. I heard there was a paying job up here, but the caterer on duty took one look and put me on her shit list. The cunt may have thought I wanted her job. Probably, I did. Anyway, I was pissed off and went to grab the elevator back down to the street, and got treated instead to a black comedy sketch." I snatch a beer from a passing kid, pop the tin's opener with my teeth, and chug it. Kid's amazed. The Stets, too.

"One of us," the short one in the orange tee says, and the tall dude agrees with a little shrug, wallowing something around in his jaws. They let me know that they have to throw a couple of pretty rough assholes off the roof, and ask if I can help.

"I doubt I can do the buggers any hurt," I say, crumpling the beercan and tossing it away, "but maybe I could offer them blow-jobs and hobble them with their own pants. Sort of how we used to do calves and ponies when neutering them."

The short one heehaws, the tall one in the western vest flashes a grin so quick you'd miss it if you blinked, and releases a gob of chaw. "That should do it," the little one hoots. "They're hard guys with guns, but guns ain't allowed up here. Without 'em, they're just a coupla soft nut trees, ready for the harvest."

"It's a done deal then, chums, but I have a favor to ask. It's that hardass caterer. I need help opening up the job market."

My buddies eyeball each other briefly. "No problem," says the little general, his oversized cowboy hat comically flattening out his big ears. Was that a declaration or a question? A command? His smiling glance makes me feel targeted. "Okie-dokie," replies the hefty young country girl in her unvarnished vernacular. "Let's get at it."

Get at what? Is something bad about to happen? As the heavy-set farm girl stamps by in her clodhoppers, she shakes her big hips and winks at me, but that doesn't make me feel any better. She has a certain rustic charm and her wink is friendly enough (I wink back in self-defense), but I'm worried now that the lovely woman who's been passing around the appetizers might be in some kind of danger. I drop my plans to go out to the roof terrace for a last glimpse of the setting sun and detour into the kitchen to tell the serving lady what I've heard.

There's a big crowd of people milling about in here, filling the kitchen to capacity, busy at all the dumb things one does at parties—drinking, flirting, exchanging big money tips, loading up on the munchies, then laughing with their mouths full, trading hugs and nose bumps and pinching each other's rearends—but she's not among them. The only working colleague of the caterer in here is the chief cook, and he's doing none of these things. He's a big grumpy man, looks foreign, is not at all playful and is even a bit frightening, his wooden crutches digging into the dark armpits of his filthy tee shirt and a permanent sneer on his round unshaven face. I hastily describe to him the country girl and her friends and the things they said, though I can't be sure he has understood any of it. At heart, he's no doubt a gentle fellow, but, from the look he's giving me, I decide to stop worrying about other people and mind my own business. If it's too late for the sunset, maybe I can still catch the moonrise.

When we first came here, my friends thought this was a groovy place for a party, but I found it too high and lonesome, and, at times, downright scary. After that awesome elevator fiasco, my friends wanted to have another crazy ride, but once was enough for me. I've lost track of them now, but they're silly girls and I don't miss them. I did manage to meet the former owners, a sweet middle-aged couple, still very lovey-dovey for their age. They were celebrating something (their anniversary maybe). We got on great. The lady asked me if I might be of help to her later on, and I said, sure. The current owner, contrarily, is a gross heavyset man with bad breath, much too quick with his grabby paws. Maybe he feels owning this property gives him certain privileges, and it might, it's a nice high-end apartment, though as its owner, he's also its prisoner, more or less obliged to throw parties like this one from time to time to make proper use of it. My friends have told me, giggling childishly, that he's an eligible bachelor, though one would have to be pretty desperate to put up with such an ugly brute, no matter how rich he is.

On my way to the terrace door, I'm nearly run over by a frantic fat man, racing around, in one door and out the other, caring not a whit who's in his way, wailing insanely about his missing sex, adding that he set it down somewhere and somebody walked off with it. No one knows what the crazy man is howling about, but whatever happened, at least the obnoxious goose honks have stopped—though what his missing sex had to do with that is anybody's guess. The goose? Maybe somebody throttled it. The poor man is an object of some pity (mine, anyway; it's a terrible thing to lose your sex) until he starts bragging obscenely about knowing best how to finger and blow his darling to get the most out of her, whereupon I tune him out—there is a certain nastiness of language that can make me physically ill—and, grabbing a couple of bites of caramelized foie gras on rice crackers from a nearby platter, I escape to the terrace.

It's not yet night, though darkness has probably fallen on the streets below and the light up here is fading fast. No sign of the moon, but people are pressing expectantly against the terrace railing, their heads tilted back, so probably it hasn't happened yet. The foie gras is fantastic, but light. I was hungry when I came here, still am. This amazing spread doesn't fill a girl up, I could eat it all night. I brush the crumbs off my hands and edge away from the others toward the darker, more anonymous part of the terrace garden, avoiding on principle all scary overlooks. A moon's a moon, after all, and should be visible, no matter where one stands.

There's someone out here dressed like a nun, or maybe she *is* a nun, certainly she smells like one. She's greeted by people who are crossing themselves while holding their noses as if it's a kind of recognition signal among them. The nun pauses to say something to a young man in pressed denims and a cashmere sweater. She slaps him fiercely on his cute backside and he hangs his head in pretend shame, or real shame, who's to say? They are being watched by a sinister man with a bushy beard, silhouetted by the garden lights behind him, making him seem more like an apparition than a real man, and I realize, as he turns to look at me, how foolish I was to come out here alone. "Don't be afraid," he says, but I *am* afraid. I hurry away, hoping he doesn't follow.

I find it less comfortable out here than I had hoped, but I'm intent on seeing the promised moonrise, my first as a city girl, and I'm glad I'm at least wearing my woolen skirt. We're very high up, *too* high, and I find myself wondering—against my will—what it must feel like to fall from such a height. Does one know what's happening *as* it's happening? Can one think at all while falling? Do you pass out before slamming into the pavement? I shiver. Awful thoughts.

And it is while I'm suffering those insufferable imaginings, that I catch a glimpse, just over the bearded man's sloped shoulders (he's still watching me!), of the serving woman I was looking for, passing out appetizers. I have to warn her about something, but for the moment I'm too shaken to remember it. Something about the market, or markets. She hurries past, glancing nervously over her shoulder at two boys in cowboy hats who, along with that farm girl I saw inside, are chasing after her. Now I remember. I try to reach her, but a chunky fellow in white pants and a gaudy plaid jacket is stupidly blocking my way.

"Let me by! This is important!" I cry. But then one of the chasing boys throws himself at the serving lady in a flying tackle, and she comes down with a fearsome bang. That does it. Such violence always makes me break out in hives. The caterer's silver tray of goodies goes sailing, as she stiff-arms the tackler and ducks into the penthouse though a door held open by the man in white pants who gets his face smacked by a sour-cherry tart for his heroics. I back off, hoping she's home free, and bump into the pernicious man with the bushy beard, who's been dogging my heels.

"It's all over," he whispers, raising goose bumps.

"The party?" I gasp.

"Everything . . . " sighs the bearded man with grave solemnity. Scares her pants off. Which are no doubt a size or two larger than the sweet young thing would wish.

I wipe the tart out of my eyes with the bar towel tossed to me by the grinning bartender (I lust for cherry-walnut pie, but not as face paint) and push in behind the stampede. An old man leans into the shifting multitudes like the Grim Reaper reaping, a long-limbed minister of the evangelical sort, one who's been spreading the Good Word on the party like rancid butter. "You are frightening the child," he says to the bearded man. She is indeed frightened and runs away. "You see?"

"I often have that effect on people," says the other with a sad disarming smile, revealing the gap in his front teeth, "having no soothing delusions to offer."

The preacher is offended. "You're a dangerous man," he snaps irritably.

Bucktooth shrugs and shows his pale palms. He's about to speak, but I don't stay to listen; I leave the old boys to their hackneyed litanies and, still blinking away the pie, follow instead the two oversize Stetsons as they forge their way into the den.

Not sure how I got up here. I remember going for a round of golf, and then something happened at the ninth tee. The country club bar is there, of course, so at the ninth tee something usually happens. I fell into a sand pit over my head there one day, came up for air, and found myself on a desert island which was also the tenth green, a delicious hallucination which included a bevy of beautiful young ladies crooning love songs, but one which all too quickly dissolved into a ceramic stool in the men's room where I sat over runny poo, forlornly humming one of the songs the girls had been singing, and worrying about how my head was working. Or not.

There's a crash and some loud yelling: the serving woman must have been brought down. The bartender, gazing impassively upon the eruption, pours drinks unflinchingly. Born squad leader. He and I have gotten on. He's kept me well-supplied from his post here in the den. One of the world's good guys. I push to the front of the boozy masses and there she is, the serving lady, down on the floor behind all the legs, her bloomers in a twist but still throwing punches, and unleashing a stream of expletives all the while. The skinny cowpoke in the tatty vest slugs her, she slugs him back. Very colorful. I like it. The two cowboys succeed in pinning her arms behind her back and hump her toward the kitchen, she kicking and screaming all the way. What are they going to do to her? It doesn't look good. I'd intervene, needing a fair maiden to protect, or else dishonor, but my knees are too wobbly. An affliction of the extreme altitude maybe.

The serving woman suddenly breaks free, lashing out in all directions. She's dynamite, too much for the cowboys, both being on the meatless side—but then a rustic dame packed into bluejeans comes in and sits on the caterer, decisively adding the weight of her substantial derriere to the fracas. The serving woman blubbers something from under all that denim about a song she wants to sing before the party's over. The cowboys, distracted by a barking break-up of their own, ignore her, but the rustic with the big butt, struggling to her feet, intercedes on the woman's behalf, saying that letting her fucking sing is the fucking least they can do, given what the fuck comes next.

Wherewith, after the farm girl has led everyone in a round of applause (I clap along with the others, feeling generous), the serving lady rises like a leaky blimp and leads everyone into the large living room with its huge collaged artwork. She announces she will sing about how she was saved, and though religious songs make my head ache, I hitch up my pants and follow her, not knowing where else to go. "There's something wrong here," exclaims an alarmed lady in an evening gown sequined with pearls. The caterer shoves past her in the doorway, knocking over a pregnant woman, who has waddled blearily into the room and now ends up on her back on the carpet, knees high, yelping with pain and indignation. "Who *is* that woman?" she cries. "What is she *doing* here? What am *I* doing here?" There's probably a way of answering such questions, but neither I nor the sequined lady knows it.

The caterer meanwhile, spotlit beneath the room's bright lights, lets fly a sad song about swooning under a balloon-like moon in June. The partygoers cheer wildly. *"That's it! That's exactly how it happened!"* the woman on the floor cries out. Can't say it does anything for me, but the caterer has a deep gravelly voice and has found an appreciative audience for it, so when she goes for an encore, no one objects. No one left to object: the cowboys have split, and when the chief cook, looking mean, came limping in on his crutches a moment ago, the wary farm girl also ducked out. "I'm outa control!" the caterer growls. "You stole my soul and left a big black hole!" The guests go crazy, hooting and hollering, bellowing out their praises, and I chime in, trying not to be the outsider that I am, but when the serving woman rhymes "Jesus" with "He's us" and "Mary" with "hairy," I decide that such sad songs I can do without.

Besides, the bartender's station is abandoned. Has he gone on the run like he told us he might? Only one way out of here, and that's down. I step around the wailing lady on the floor (woops, kicked a boob, can't help it) and race for the elevator in the entrance hall—and, yes, there he is. He's thrown off his leather apron, and is carrying a fifth of whiskey and a statuette of a naked chick. Clearly has his priorities right. The statuette looks something like the golf trophy I was competing for down below: same jade buttocks, bare and buffed to a shine. I reached the ninth hole at the end of the first round, stopped in at the clubhouse bar for a quickie, and somehow wound up here on the roof of a city apartment building. Maybe I had a few quickies. Now: only a bottomless thirst.

The barman is ignoring all the shell-shocked people stumbling out of the main elevator, with expressions of puzzled terror in their eyes, and is jogging directly to the service elevator. Signals to me to follow him and I do, eager to escape this creepshow and get back to wherever I was before. He's older than me, and probably smarter. "I'm going with you, man!" shouts that skinny guy in the big cowboy hat, who's been bossing everybody around. The barman nods, jumps into the elevator, and we follow. It's roomy, but the other two pop anyone who tries to push in, so I pop a few just to establish my credentials.

As we slowly descend, the barman twists the top off the whiskey, takes a deep draft, passes the bottle to the cowboy, confessing as he does so, his goatee wagging, that heights like this wig him out. "It's a decent gig," he says, breathing heavily, "but this roof-topper is driving me nuts."

The cowboy nods sagaciously. "Same thing happened to the guy I came to this shit scene with. He was a great buddy, but plain stupid," he says. "His green dick was bugging him so bad he wanted to off himself, and I reminded him that, if you're dead, man, you can't kill anything, but he'd stopped listening, the dumbass." He drinks deeply, wipes the tears away. Green dick? "Walked off the edge, got what he'd always whined for."

The barman claps his hand over his mouth like he's about to throw up. To distract him, I ask him what he's got in his other hand. "Nameplate off the piano," he groans. He holds it out so I can see it. Not a naked chick as I'd hoped. Some kind of guitar. "Didn't come off easy," he says, still the color of the cowboy buddy's dick, "especially with that long-haired nutter banging away on the fucking keys all the time."

When the cowboy passes me the bottle, I hike my golfing pants over my pot, take a long swig, and tell them I was playing a space wars video game, when the game turned real and, not knowing how to drive the damned space ship, I crash-landed up here. I expect them to laugh at that, but they get mean, take the bottle away. The cowboy wants to know why I wasn't wearing a space suit and helmet. I tell him that when I reentered the earth's atmosphere, those things disintegrated on me. "Left me in my birthday suit, which is not top of the line. These duds I'm wearing," I add, "are a gift from a passing stranger, which he, ah, lost in the rough at the tenth hole." They grin, nod, hand me the bottle back.

I want to ask them what they think this party is all about, but the elevator comes to a sudden halt, the doors still slapped up tight against each other. Total silence, though we're listening hard with all our ears. "We must be between floors," the barman whispers, and takes up a crowbar he finds at his feet. Working together, he and the cowboy shove the crow between the doors, forcing them apart an inch or two, and eventually, surrendering, the doors slide open with a sigh, revealing a brick wall, solid except for a small gap at the bottom. They volunteer me to crawl through, though they're both skinnier than me, probably figuring that if fatass can make it, they can. The barman chips away at the hole with the crowbar, and it's tight, but by taking off my belt and pants, I can scrape through. I feel like a pioneer, crossing the last range of mountains, clawed front and back by wild bears. I turn to lend them a hand and maybe get my white golf pants back, and the elevator drops with a whistle and, eventually, a distant crash. Lucky it didn't take my arm with it.

I'm left in a dark stairwell, bare-ass like in my made-up story and all alone. Can't help feeling resentful. I'm a good guy, I deserve better. I can make out stairs going down, others going up. Down's the way home. A few steps in that direction, I find a door. I push on it, but something's blocking it. A body? No, only a snoring drunk. Two guys come to haul the drunk away. The two I was on the elevator with. They're both badly beat-up, the cowboy's Stetson crushed, the former barman missing a couple of front teeth, his pants ripped. They're clearly pissed about something, don't even acknowledge my presence when I slap their shoulders in greeting, other than to scowl disapprovingly at my limp dick. They load the drunk onto a blanket.

Huge pack-up, much as I left the penthouse overhead. If it is overhead. That knocked-up lady is there lying on the floor with her knees up, the caterer is still exercising her vocal cords, the silver-haired preacher is god-blessing everybody. It's weird. I back out, run up the stairs (stairs?) past the broken elevator (is this a rooftop penthouse, or what?), bump the door open at the top of the staircase with my naked rump. No passed-out body blocking the door this time, but everybody else is there like before: the beardy joker, the lady on the floor screaming that her water is breaking, the ancient cripple on a cane, the skinny old evangelical preacher, the sweating serving lady in the frilly apron, even the skinny cowpoke in the crushed hat and the battered ex-barman, now hauling their loaded blanket out a door, bumping it along. I feel like I'm acting out a nightmare. An obese woman reaches under her skirt and peels down her panties, hands them to me. The preacher bears down on me like a vulture. I shove him away with one hand, the other struggling with the underwear, but I stay my ground. "Make your peace with the Lord," I tell him, "before it's too late!"

He bristles and I wait for the anticipated blow, but it is he who backs down, staring confusedly at a hand wrapped in silk. I have often felt the Divine Being nearby, though never so near as at this moment. I have always drawn close to Him, or as close as I dared, and we have spoken then, or at least I spoke, certain that He was listening and judging the sincerity of my love for Him. I have never fawned, never groveled. He is the Lord, but He is one who loathes servility, extols the independent spirit, which, as everyone knows, I have always exemplified.

When I confess to others my devotion to the Lord, I speak with an eloquence meant to stir passions on behalf of the Divinity I adore, although, as readers of my seminal book, *The Healing Powers of Doubt*, are well aware, at critical moments in my long life, I have harbored fundamental misgivings about His very Being. Today, those misgivings reached a new nadir, enveloping me in an unfathomable darkness, yet tonight, thanks to a holy nun, what few uncertainties might yet have been lurking in the shadowy recesses of my soul, have been for all time—*for all time!*—utterly extirpated. Through her, He has found me. He has entered transcendentally into me like a vapor passes into an absorbent tissue, a spilled fluid into a sponge, like smoke into the forgiving air. I am His.

But whence came He? Strangely, by way of this half-naked foul-mouthed fellow who burst into the room so obscenely. The ways of the Lord are indeed most mysterious. I seemed to *feel* the fellow's shove before he actually laid a hand on me, and then the Lord passed into me and took lodging in my soul, not as an invasion, not as a haunting, but like a sudden realization. Is He the same Divinity I once adored? Of course He is. There cannot be two infinite Beings in the only space we humanly know. No matter the route by which, grown massive in density, even while withering to a point, He found me, where He leads now, I must follow. No more abstemious preparations. He is both without—this entire festive occasion participates in His Being, all the *world* does—and within. We are one. I prayed to Him that the young man be provided more suitable apparel and my prayer has been answered. Everything coheres!

Oh what a joy the miracle of life is! What a delight! Death, too, being but life's joyful climax! Why can all not see it so? Why do so many choose instead a gloomier view as though feeding the devil's appetite? It's simple: they have denied the Lord's embrace! Not I! When the Divinity summons forth His holy beings, freed of all earthly encumbrances, to join Him in His ecstatic dance of life—yes, *dance!* the holy dance of saints, of angels—thanks to that blessèd nun, who tonight has become my dear friend and mentor, my partner in the dance of life, I will be there, my sinful body, even if old and crippled, free at last!

It is she who has guided me from the errant waywardness of the mind to the true holiness of the body, not as a sensualist, but as one aware of what it means to be alive in the Lord's physical world. I too was once a captive of the Word, having sought always to *think* my way to the Lord, convinced at times that such wisdom was a kind of sickness, but she has opened my eyes to the physical embodiment, the sacred sanctuary, of the Divine Spirit. Though there are many who denigrate her and call her names, some too vulgar to repeat, I see as well that I am not alone in having enjoyed her visionary gifts. She has left her wholesome mark on many, some of whom claim to have attended her private séances and to have taken communion with her.

Among her followers, a greeting of sorts has sprung up tonight, consisting of crossing oneself while pinching one's nose, and I adopt that when soliciting information regarding her whereabouts. I am eager now to meet once more with her to ask if this is the usual manner by which the Lord is received by sinners such as I. I follow her familiar odor into the grand reception room, where last I saw her, but, though it is packed with people and her powerful fragrance saturates the room, she herself is nowhere to be seen.

Why am I here? An existential question deserving of an existential answer: to wit, I don't know. I only know that when I saw the pinned-up invitation, I felt compelled, having lost the faith that had sustained and guided me for so long, to accept it. There are secondary reasons of course. Despair drives one to many unwise decisions. The invitation was to a party and, in my dissolute and faithless state of mind, that had a certain false appeal: libertinism, followed eventually by hurling the sin-ridden body from this high place into the beyond. I have always had particular good fortune in consoling ladies who have taken on too much weight, of which fortunately, for this poor sinner, there are a great many, and at parties, not least of all. There were indeed some on the elevator up to the penthouse, and I was led to believe, as I was forced to rub up against them, that I might yet enjoy more intimately their company as a farewell offering.

But then, beyond the fat ladies, I chanced to see the holy nun, dressed in all her saintly regalia, also taking the elevator to the penthouse. It was me she was looking at. I nearly said, "looking *through*," for that is what it felt like. I had the strange sensation that I was the only reason in fact that she was on the elevator, and it was my salvation alone that she sought. She seemed to be castigating me for my woeful thoughts, yet also alerting me to the body's essential worthiness. Her arms were folded, both hands gripping her upper arms, yet she seemed to reach past all the others to bless my manhood, as though to say: this, too, is worthy of adoration, and it returned her worship her as best it could. I longed for meaning in my life and the nun showed me the way.

One entire wall of this room is devoted to a very beautiful work of art, composed of a cascade of small photographs, each revealing some aspect of daily life. The variety of the imagery calls reality itself into question and presses upon the viewer the need to make choices within that unstable reality. Though this remarkable collage goes largely unattended by the other party-goers, one feels in it the presence of the Lord, and I say so to a gentleman standing nearby.

"It's a vision of hell," he says chillingly.

"Some of the photographs the artist employed are indeed quite painful to behold," I reply, searching for a brilliance equal to that of the artwork we are discussing, "but together they constitute a joyful celebration of the totality of the human experience. It is a noble work of artistic genius that makes one feel the presence of something far grander than oneself. It is nothing less than a sacred oracle!"

"Bull," says my interlocutor, at a loss for a more elegant reply, equal to my own. "Look at those images of the woman slicing her own eyeballs or that poor man emasculating himself, all in the name of your Lord! It's terrifying! What the collage celebrates is plain madness!"

"That may be so," I say, "true zeal being a divine form of madness." Though the fellow is clearly disinclined to engage in meaningful discourse, I persist, aware that others have joined us, as though to test me. Is the holy nun among them? I will not be found wanting. "I know, as the artist knew, that the blesséd Divinity is less benign than perhaps one might hope. He is the Lord of the Universe, after all, so of *course* He can be terrifying. People must die, after all, to be spiritually conjoined with Him." "What a nightmare! Your blesséd Divinity is an appalling anti-human tyrant."

"I *agree* with you that He is not human. But, far from being *anti*-human, He is the Good Father, holding our hand on the hard passage through life and the final crisis of death. He is my beacon. I shall follow Him to the end of the earth." I'm not sure what I mean by that, but I assume it has to do with making a climactic exit. My congregations, past and future, call out to me. The sweet nun, too. I hear her. "Whither go I, blindly if need be, I know the Divinity will take care of me," I announce loudly to the gentleman and to the world, and off he struts toward the entrance hall. *Oh no!* He's headed for the doorway under the EXIT sign that lawyer and his woman disappeared through!

"*Wait!*" I cry, rushing forward. "*There are no stairs—!*" Too late! He's through the door! The last I see of him is his silvery shock of hair as it drops below the threshold, the door silently closing above him. He trusted his imaginary divinity. Poor judgment. Like signing up with the wrong dance partner, the one who has gone home early, to call up an old metaphor from my own generation, a metaphor perhaps too frivolous for the occasion.

Have I provoked that old fool's leap into oblivion with my frivolity? Possibly, but one can feel only grief, not guilt, for speaking, even if jokingly, of the way the cosmos operates, oblivion being the inescapable outcome, and it doesn't much matter when or how that happens. And yet I do feel something *like* guilt, simply for acknowledging the truth, as though there were something wicked about truth itself, just as there seems to be something wicked about the exercise of reason, wickedness being another word for our aberrant evolution. Maybe, like all the other creatures of the earth, we are not meant to comprehend our circumstances, such comprehension condemning us to a vision that might impair our will to go on prolonging the catastrophe. Bees and termites, free of oversized brains that ask unanswerable questions, are completely ignorant of their circumstances and do very nicely. Though, what do I mean (there I go again) by "meant?" Are perceptions of design just another form of wickedness? Of frivolity? Somehow I feel myself swarming around my own sorry self.

Swarm intelligence, as I tell my students, is the opposite of consciousness. It emerges from the programmed interaction of individuals without a control center, and, in humans, leads to behavior governed by willful stupidity. Fade out, play golf, get a buzz on, follow the leader. Sometimes accompanied by cool rhythms that pleasurably activate one's bobble head. What else-where gets tagged as "collective effervescence," experienced at religious ingatherings, political rallies, rock concerts, drunken parties. Hard to resist. Feels too good. Ignore reality. Hang out in the frothy swarm.

My students, for the most part, once they escape the restraints of the classroom, do just that. Their favorite party game this year is tag sex. It's fun, mostly mindless, swarm-friendly. The game pretty much plays itself once everyone's clothes are off and the masks are on, and generates a kind of dour happiness. That's my experience anyway; for the young, having little or nothing as yet to regret, it's probably less dour in the main. They don't like old guys like me to join in, scared by the baggy wrinkles maybe, something of a downer for me as well, but I have research to do. We sometimes talk about it in class the next day. Always triggers a lot of giddy laughter. The old prof with a warped hard-on under his sagging belly: Imagine!

But my investigation of swarm intelligence, if a tad obses-sive and maybe even silly, has a practical purpose. There's a book underway; an essay from it has already been published. I suspect it's why I'm here tonight, though I have no idea about the mechanics of this party, nor remember who or what drew me here, even how I found out about it. An invitation? There's a vague memory of one, but vague memories are not to be trusted. I have a thousand such memories of youthful joy, for example, which I know to be nothing more than wistful imaginings, powered by momentary stirrings of the gonads. There is a time in life when happiness, so-called, is as free as the air, and a time when it is taken away.

In spite of all the telltale aromas, few of my mostly happy students seem to be here tonight; a good thing, seeing the direction the party seems to be taking. That gang of tough girls, following me up, has crashed the party, but none of my favorites. I miss them. Though I treat them all as colleagues, they are younger colleagues, and so can be lectured to as well as conversed with, and I do feel in lecture-mode tonight, with the need therefore of an attentive audience. I would like to tell them, for example, about how the hive instinct feels like a real haunting, an intrusive force that infects thought and alters behavior, but that has no explanation, scientific, theological, or otherwise: that terrifying anti-human divinity that drove the old evangelical preacher to his leap into oblivion.

Given the way the elevator is working, or not working (guests are still arriving, but none so far as I can tell are leaving, except in the grotesque manner that that frenzied couple and the preacher left), pursuing the book idea may no longer be entirely relevant. But irrelevance has never stopped me before, much to my frequent discredit, nor is it likely to stop me now. The book about swarm intelligence is the game I am playing. The game that remains.

Earlier, I had a brief conversation with an eccentric man, more or less my age. I asked him what *his* game was and, smiling toothily through his thick beard, white with streaks of red, he told me he was an artist of sorts, one who crafted love, wisdom, and confidence among his fellow human beings. I laughed and said I looked forward to seeing his finished artworks hanging in the museum. He studied me soberly for a long moment. It's true, he said. Nothing deflects the horror like senseless wit. He chewed on his beard a moment, prolonging his annoying study, then slowly walked away, pursued by a wide-bottomed woman with a lilac bow in her hair. I felt resentful, like an inappropriately disciplined child.

Now, I may have a second shot at him. He has passed by, amid a crowd of whooping party guests, he the only sober one, on their way into the kitchen, thence to the roof terrace, with the shouted intention of witnessing the moonrise. I follow, plotting out the contours of a conversation with him, one perhaps focused on my field of expertise, by way of the compelling lure of setting suns, a useful metaphor, not merely for the aging process (the sun sets for all of us), but also for the way free thinking can slip into forgetfulness and darkness.

In the kitchen, however, I find the chief cook, on his knees behind the large industrial oven, a smelly black cigarette between his teeth, pummeling a limp half-conscious man, who might be (his bloodied face is unrecognizable) one of the new owners of this penthouse, and I pause to caution the chef, resting my hand on his crisp white sleeve. "Easy, friend, you'll spoil his good looks!" Surprised by my hand, he does let up, allowing his battered victim to crawl away as he rises unsteadily to his feet, flicking away his smoke, his offended gaze, under his Yorkshire-pudding topper, now turned on me. I notice for the first time the others who are with him, now stepping out of the shadows, some young men and women roughly the age of my students. One of the boys pushes his bookworm spectacles up on the bridge of his skinny nose (always happy, in such a locale as this, to spy one of my own), and it promptly slides back down again. I give him a sympathetic smile, thinking about the many inconsequential ways the world can disappoint a person, when a longhaired stringbean rudely grabs my arm. I know I should remain professorially above it all, but to pass seamlessly from the comedy of thought to that of action, I brush him off, shouting jokingly: "Fuck off!" and the chief cook lands a haymaker on the elitist professor's smirking jaw that almost takes his head off. The cook, I've been told, is a famous but disgraced boxer, and, clearly, he could still hold his own in the fighting business. They're proud of him. *I'm* proud of him.

The man he has knocked out is a godless leftwing professor who is said by others at the party to have danced stark naked with his students, boys and girls alike. Those who told me were grinning as if telling a dirty joke, but such behavior is as disgusting as it is dangerous, and I say so to the honorable lady who befriended me earlier. "Children at that age are so vulnerable!" I shout over the noisy twaddle of the party guests, streaming through on their way out to the roof terrace, none seeming overly concerned about the recent altercation. The lady agrees with me, nodding at two young men, one in a wide-brimmed cowboy hat, his partner a long-haired musician, dressed in a worn but handsome black suit with a black clip-on bowtie like my own more colorful polka-dotted one. They lift the professor's lifeless body like a sack of potatoes and cart it out the door.

The lady came to my rescue a short time ago, when I was set upon by a gang of tough young women, some of whom are here tonight. They were laboring under the misconception that I was a member of their own sex and were trying to pull my pants down to prove it. They were stopped by the lady, then still a stranger, who proposed that I should simply expose myself to them to shut them up. I declined, confessing in a whisper that I was embarrassingly underendowed, so she whispered back that, if I allowed her to see for herself, we could satisfy everyone. She was considerably older than me and had a commanding presence not unlike that of a doctor, so, somewhat boxed in and feeling a peculiar compulsion to do so, I surrendered my privacy to her. After reaching into my trousers to feel about, gasping slightly as if in disbelief (her delicate hand felt like a little animal in there), she sternly reprimanded the young women for their rude behavior, then brought me here, just in time to witness Cookie's stunning punch (which I felt sympathetically as a mild disturbance near where her hand had been), to meet some of the law-and-order people she has been assembling. I am happy to have been welcomed into their midst and to have won the affection of their leader. It has made the party, a puzzle to me all night, seem less strange and foreboding.

The leader introduces me now to Cookie, a stout gentleman on crutches, and I express my gratitude, on behalf of all right-thinking persons, for his decisive intervention; he grunts menacingly in response, lighting up afresh, and I decide to say no more. The woman takes me aside to tell me that he once had a promising pugilistic career, until the day, she explains, his manager ordered him to throw a fight. "The unmerciful teasing by hecklers at that bout caused him to lose his equanimity, and, in a fit of anger, he destroyed his opponent with a powerful blow not unlike the one that knocked out the professor. He wasn't supposed to do that, and several influential high-stakes gamblers, who had wagered heavily on the contest, lost their shirts, as they say on the street. While he was at it, he unleashed his fury on his treacherous manager as well, who also did not survive."

I acknowledge all of this with a nod of understanding, grateful for her confidence, so freely given. "He was sent to prison for murder, having no one to defend him," she continues, "and, when he was released a few years later, some brutish men were waiting for him. They beat him severely and broke both his legs, and no doubt would have broken his arms as well, but they needed his signature on a few documents. He defaced the documents with large X's, but as he was a foreigner, the X's were accepted as signatures. That, anyway, is the sad story he has told me in his clumsy manner. To this day, as you can see, his legs remain largely useless, and his frequent wincing suggests he is in constant pain, though he never complains." Good, I thought, stroking my small square moustache meditatively, and I shall never complain either. "He was never the brightest of men, but he is a valiant trooper for our cause, an inspirational cause that in turn has somewhat restored his spirits. Thanks to adopting our militant beliefs, he is a new man. And, as evidence of his renewed spirit, his appetizers tonight have been simply marvelous!" As indeed they have. I accept another as it passes by. So light!

I thank her for all the good she is doing in the world, and, in farewell, offer her my services. She points to an older bearded man and says there is indeed something I could do for the movement. She often speaks of their team as a "squad," carrying out the will of the people, frequently borrowing military terms to describe who they are and what they do. The longhaired musician, yelled at obscenely by the professor, for example, is called "a good soldier" by the woman. I feel that I also want to be a good soldier, and she says one of the best ways to do that is to keep an eye for her on that man with the bushy beard. She always thought of him as a mental defective, but others seem to be heeding him, and he may have to be reassessed. I promise to do that, happy to be of some practical use to the good lady and to her "squad."

The musician reminds me of a childhood friend, a thin wiry girl who at the time was studying the violin, and I am consequently overtaken by a feeling toward him of nostalgic tenderness. Something in the way his hair hangs over his face in unwashed gobbets, shyly hiding his gaze and much of the rest of his visage as well; perhaps, like the little girl, he has prominent front teeth. She was a very independent child, free and excitable, but utterly devoted to her instrument, as I was to ideation, and we soon developed a sympathetic bond. Like me, she was quite religious, though neither of us were so in an entirely conventional way, her religion being fortified by music, sacred music in particular, as mine was by thought, specifically theological thought, and we developed a chaste relationship that, though childish, was both profound and enduring. Had she not ended her life prematurely, after being brutally raped by her violin teacher (who also died a sorry death, said to have been at the hands of another of his students, a never-proven act of jealousy; only I know how it really happened), we would probably still be together, and I would not be suffering these paralyzing attacks of loneliness.

It is my hope to recover something of that ennobling relationship, still aglow in my memory, by way of my newfound alliances, so when at last I meet the contrabassist in the noisy music room, it is deep rapport—not mere friendship—that I am seeking.

And indeed, almost immediately, we find ourselves speaking of ultimate matters, just as the violinist and I so often did. We agree that Being is not friendly toward man, and I tell him, raising my voice above the chatter and clink of glasses, that I have faith that there must be a better world and that I wish to be taken there.

"Yep, the one we're in is definitely in the final stages of rigor mortis," he replies. "I've often wished the same thing as you, but with zero expectations, having no belief in other worlds. There's only this shit world we're in, with death at the end of it."

"Perhaps some will be spared. Don't you hope to be one of them?"

"No hope at all. But I still want to see more things, do more things, before the fucker ends."

I push my glasses up the treacherous slope of my nose, and the bassist laughs as it slips down again, sliding his finger mockingly down a sounded string. It is not a hostile laugh, it's more like a laugh of recognition, warm and friendly, and I laugh along with him. I am conversing, as I have often done, with a nihilist, and I know that, with patience and understanding, there are ways to soften their hostile opinions. "In the sphere," I begin, "of perfect harmony—"

"Doesn't exist," the bassist interrupts. "Pipe dream. Speaking of which," he adds, tapping his jacket pocket, "I deal in them. Any time you want a hit . . . "

"No, thank you, but—"

"That's a cool jacket," he says, caressing the black chamois.

I press on, having faith in my rescuer's judgment about his loyalty and integrity—she spoke so highly of him!—but his fondling of my jacket is making me uncomfortable. "But what *do* you believe in?"

"I believe in what's in there," says the bassist, pointing, and he grins, adding mischievously: "That witch lady said it's the cutest little thing."

"She did?" I gasp, pushing his hand away from my fly.

"C'mon, just a little peeksie?"

"*NO!*" Things are not happening as I thought they might. I lurch away, crashing into some clumsy fool, at the very moment I enter the room, not the right one obviously, looking for the little bar (great selection, hard to know where to start), when—*BAM!*—something like a runaway train strikes me down and rumbles right over me. *Foo!* "If you need any pipe dreams, let me know. I'm the man to see," someone calls out, and from the floor I raise my hand: "Count me in!"

I feel something left over from the impact like gas on the stomach, so I lie there a moment, happily thinking my own little thoughts, and working up a meditative fart or two. The farts pop out easily enough, but they don't ease the pressure, so finally, to avoid being stepped on, I just pick myself up. It wasn't very pleasant, getting run over, but such things happen at parties. Best to get numb enough not to feel anything, and I'm nearly there. Still farting, though—now that I've started, I can't seem to stop. I find a redheaded lady too deep in her cups to notice the little poopety-poops, and ask her where the bar's gone to. The good soul crosses her eyes and points back over my shoulder.

Turns out it's in the room I was just walking out of. I must have missed it. Same little family bar, same noisy mob of impatient boozehounds, but no bartender. I take advantage of that, pushing into the melee to grab up a half-empty gin bottle on the bar, taking a couple of quick gulps straight from the neck. Hah. Needed that. Did anyone see me? If they did, they don't seem to care. I pour the remaining gin into a water glass, fish some ice out of someone's abandoned drink. I can still stand, just. Can't hit the glass with the ice cubes, though. I screw the top off a fresh bottle, and wink at whomever, fart for the pleasure of it, and then again, more emphatically, opening a path out of the pack-up.

Powered by the chugging farts, I drift into the next room, the one I was heading for in the first place, hoping it might have a bed in it. It doesn't. What it has is a grand piano. Something one could stretch out on, but there's some guy with knotty pigtails using it as a noisemaker. Have I been in here before? Probably. The pig-tailed piano pounder is joined by a sax player who's bouncing about the room leaping on lightbulbs, while blowing annoyingly loud burping noises. He says the bulbs must be made of lead.

Crazy. It's that kind of party. There's a shiny little stone doll in a corner, looking lonesome. I pocket her, planning to return her to her rightful owner, who's probably forgotten where he or she put her, if I see them, and then stagger into the adjoining room, searching for someone to cast my fading smile upon.

What I find is another party guy like myself, a jolly good-hearted fellow, wearing a conviviality he was likely born with, a chunky little guy with slicked-down blond hair, thinning out on top, who agrees with everything I say. I feel better. "I'm here for the booze," I say, laughing, and he laughs and says he is, too. We clink glasses, and he laughs at that as well. "All my life, I've worked hard at being a good guy," I say, farting noisily. "It's not fair." For some reason, he thinks that's pretty funny, though I don't even know what I mean. "What's fair?" he asks, guffaw-ing. "What's *not* fair," I laugh. I'm farting merrily and we're both whooping and slapping each other's shoulders and pouring more drinks. I ask him how he found out about the party, and he says the little lady dragged him to it. I'm not sure if he's talking about his wife or some other. He's not sure either, he just snorts with laughter when I ask him. "She's in there, bless her heart," he howls, pointing toward some other room, maybe some other party, "tossing drinks down like sugared tea!" For some rea-son, that strikes *me* as hilarious—"Sugared *tea!*"—and I laugh so hard I risk falling over. When I've recovered my balance, I tell him this party is a rationalist's fucking nightmare, and he says, "You know how you can always recognize a rationalist? They're all *drunks!*" Then he breaks into a wheezing tears-in-his-eyes laugh, like he's just said something unbelievably funny, so I laugh along with him because maybe he has. "I know what you mean," I say, and he doubles up again with wild convulsions. I love this guy.

Whereupon, as though announced by my little fanfare, we are joined by a gorgeous woman who is also laughing, though less uproariously, wanting to know what's so funny. I don't know if it's his little lady, but probably not, because he doesn't seem to recognize her. He winks at me and gestures as though to suggest she's a hot ticket. "Built like a brick bathroom!" he snorts, hiding his mouth behind a chubby hand. The brick bathroom is laughing generously, but there's something dark about her laughter, as though she knows too much to be able to let herself go. I'm drawn to that and by now I'm making my moves. But it's the little guy I've been talking with she's after. She strokes his flushed face, giggles, pulls teasingly on his crotch as he twists away in wheezing embarrassment. He's still laughing, but also peering around for help. I push him out of the way.

"I know what you mean," I say, apropos of nothing. The guy is still whooping with tears in his eyes like it's the biggest joke ever, but the woman has stopped laughing and is locking in on my gaze. I feel like one chosen. The farts are now coming, one after the other, purring like a little motor, but she doesn't seem to mind. She hugs me tightly, pumping them out. We kiss. It's very intense. My little fart-motor is cranked up full-throttle. We're stumbling awkwardly in a weird sort of dance toward a bedroom door that says EXIT. A bedroom door shouldn't say that. She's trembling with excitement. "I'm terribly sorry! It's just that I suddenly know what's happening up here," she whispers breathlessly in my ear. "There's only one way out. It's scary. I need company." What—?

If anything is sacred in this world, it's a lover's privacy, so when the couple moves in a frantic clinch toward a bedroom door, even if they're only having a partytime one-off, I discreetly turn away—and at the same moment I suddenly feel someone intruding on *my* privacy by sticking a *thumb* in me, or *worse!* I slap at my skirt and spin around: there's no one there, not even those two lovers, nothing but a closing door. The sensation is gone, maybe never was. *Felt* real, but sensations can't be trusted, not up here. This is, to say the least, a very peculiar place, enough so to make a girl sometimes doubt her sanity.

They must have seen me coming: victim of the day. I say "they," though in fact I found my ticket on the street. *Put* there by someone? Maybe. After a taped-up invitation and a free elevator ride, there was no one at the top to take tickets; people laughed when I asked if there was one. Free food and drink, too.

But not only are the rooms all different, they're different each time I visit them. Sometimes there's an open fire in the kitchen for grilling meat and fish, for example, and then sometimes there's not. I thought there might be more than one kitchen, but the same big guy on crutches is the chef in both, if "both" is the right word. Must be done with mirrors. She reasons hopefully . . .

When I first came up here to what my ticket called a "fun house," there was a pregnant lady sprawled on the carpet in here, and she's still there, circled about by drunks, egging on her labor. "*PUSH! PUSH!!*" they shout. "Where's my husband? I thought we were going to the—*grunt!*—hospital," the poor lady whimpers, spreading her thighs and pushing as requested. Is this a fun house exhibit? "Birth and death, the two great ego trips," a bearded man remarks solemnly at my elbow, but the atmosphere is not solemn at all. Everyone is laughing, pressing forward to get a better view. A heavy-browed man with a ring in his nose, scowling and grinning at the same time, elbows his way in and, taking his half-eaten cigar out of his fat lips, adds his booming voice to the "*PUSH! PUSH!*" chorus. A gushy excitable woman with her hand squeezed between her thighs, gazes wide-eyed at the lady on the floor and says she just *loves* this wild high-in-the-sky party; an old roué strokes her backside and whispers something in her ear that makes her squeal. Maybe they're all actors, only pretending.

Though my ticket allows it, I choose not to photograph the lady (where is the father?), grabbing instead a few details from the massive collage of old black-and-white prints covering one wall, an artwork too big for my little phone camera to take in whole, even with the zoom-back at max, but it's intriguing. The black bits can be seen, with a modest stretch of the imagination, as a line drawing of a face, the white parts the skull underneath, though maybe I'm seeing only what my morbid imagination wants to see.

Since arriving, I've gone room by room, photographing the apartment and, only incidentally, the guests. Places, not people, that's me. The smoke-filled rooms, not the smokers. The fun house, not the fun. I remember when it was such a big deal to be a photographer. Now everybody's one, even me. This is a party, with all that that implies, so I've steered clear, as best I can, of bedrooms and bathrooms. Doors lead to other rooms, but there's no guessing as to what's on the other side. A kitchen can be off a bedroom, and when one returns to the kitchen, it may not still *be* a kitchen. When in one bathroom I was startled by two naked people sharing a shower, I backed out and found myself in *another* bathroom, this one with an old woman on the stool. She asked me for some toilet paper.

I took snaps and videos of the music room, the kitchen, family rooms, bathrooms (the oddest *human* thing was a rather proper lady applying a creamy lotion to a shirtless young man's bright green genitalia; I didn't photograph it or him, though I have to admit the green parts invited cameras), various dining rooms, hallways, a television room, a gymnasium, a powder room, a small one-lane bowling alley, and several game rooms, one just for playing cards in foursomes, another for solitaire, one for adult party games, and yet another for putting picture puzzles together; I photographed a couple of the less risqué completed puzzles. The tour has been well worth the ticket price, whoever paid it; if.

But, as I discover, thousands of snapshots and videos too late, the camera on my phone isn't recording anything. Always an amateur, stupidly ignorant of my own equipment! At first,

I suppose it's some set-up mistake I've made or the battery's dead, but it turns out that everyone up here has the same problem. Most don't really care—photos can be less than flattering, after all, even incriminating—but for me, it's a professional crisis. In the end, I decide I need the viewfinder even more than the captured images, so, arousing the curiosity of everyone, I go on using the camera to tell me what I'm looking at on my explorations, seeing on the little screen—zooming in, zooming out—all I can while I can.

What I see now on that tiny screen is a pair of double doors with a sign on them that says THEATER. This is exciting. There is nothing on my ticket that says the penthouse has its own theater. But when I look away from the phone, I'm in the room I was in before, packed full of people, and the double doors aren't there. The viewfinder still sees them, however, so, using it as my guide, I walk out onto the roof terrace toward the screen image, stepping around the people and objects in the way, all I've seen so far prepping me for this strange exercise. I zoom in on the door handles and my enlarged hands, rings and all, appear on the little screen, reaching for them. I open them and push on in.

The lobby of the theater is dark as is its small auditorium, but I can see now, about six rows back, a bald-headed man with a jutting chin, tape holding together the temple arms of his spectacles. He's using a penlight to read from a little notebook. I am no longer looking at the cellphone screen; he's there and I walk toward him, slip into the row of seats behind him. He mumbles, perhaps to me, perhaps only reading aloud what he has written: "Someone has said, in a place like this, that life is a dream. One can only hope that, however brief and meaningless the dream, waking up doesn't hurt too much." I shudder, wondering at the ripple of momentary dread his weirdly clumsy words have stirred. He's a somewhat bent and wizened man, but may not be as old as he looks. "In my play about it," he says, "the body is the stage, the driving action sex, the play itself that action's preludes and postludes. But the *meaning* of the performance lies elsewhere . . ."

"Why, it's a dream play about *love!*" I exclaim, surprising myself.

He turns to look at me, squinting through his cracked bifocals. "No, it's a realistic play about zombies," he says in a cold echoey voice. Omigod! *He's a crazy man!*

"I do sometimes think of all these party people as the walking dead," I say tentatively, wondering if I should get up and run, "though I'm not sure who they really repre—"

"WATCH!" he roars, making me jump. It's like night in here, what am I supposed to be watching, for pete's sake? Is he mad about something? How can he see anything at all through those broken specs? "They're rising from their tombs and dancing, their bones rattling hollowly!" Rising from their *what?* Good grief! He's a deep voice boomer, on top of being a nut case! I feel an alarming flutter in my bosom! Is this a play or what? "O rattle them bones!" I myself call forth the dead from their graves in my trademark basso profundo, and an airy whisper meant to scare the hell out of this double-chinned idiot who has deigned to interrupt my solemn meditations: "Them *damn* bones!" The line requires a xylophone. Don't have one. A rap on the back of the seat in front of me is the best I can do. But con brio: "It's a *danse macabre!*"

I scare myself, but not the bloodless intruder. The taped spectacles probably produce a contrary effect. "Oh, I see. It's a comedy, then," she says, fanning herself with a handkerchief.

"It's a tragedy," I snap angrily, somewhat deflated. It might help to have an intimidating beard like the one sported by that peculiar fellow I met earlier tonight, himself a mad scribbler of some ilk, but when I tried to grow one, all that appeared on my chin was this scatter of ridiculous threads. I might have added that this *memento mori* is intended to display the terrible emptiness that descends on life when all hope has evaporated, but I choose silence, wishing her far away. I have come here, seeking sanctuary from the oppressive festivities in the high-rise rooftop apartment, and this woman, a large bespectacled lady "of a certain age," as they say, brings only chaos and confusion—*tohu* and *bohu*, those grim companions of ancient vintage. "Be *gone*, dear lady!" I bellow suddenly in my directorial voice, making her squeak with surprise. She exits as commanded, in utter chagrin.

I say, "I have come here," though to tell the truth, here came to me, providing a sanctuary I wasn't seeking, but have found to my liking. It is hushed and shadowy, "a dark place," suiting my present temper. I had paused in my vocation of enlightening the world by way of terrifying it, to withdraw for a moment of creative meditation, and when I opened my eyes to return to "reality," lo, I was in this unlit in-house theater, filled only with an eloquent silence. This must be what is termed intuitive percipience, for I was indeed thinking theatrical thoughts, placing people I spoke with in exemplary situations fit for the small empty stage now before me.

There was, for example, before my withdrawal, a bold-bellied woman sprawled on a carpeted floor, plump knees spread, about to drop another innocent creature into the mess, and there was a cynical professor ogling her—or, at least in my mind's eye, he was ogling her—and I imagined a musical dialogue between them on the perverse instinct for survival versus the equally perverse reproductive instinct. The two instincts are, arguably, the same thing, bitter reactions to the systemic loneliness that pervades our miserable lives, but they do not feel like the same thing when one is facing rampant genitalia on the one hand and a cocked revolver on the other. So, in my script, I had the lady wailing in terror about the latter, even as the professor, penis sorrowfully in hand, expresses the former, the crowd around them chanting chorally, "*PUSH! PUSH!*"—and then I had them switch, each singing, word for word, the other's verses.

A brilliant idea in the abstract, the choral chant especially, but it's difficult for actors to perform from recumbent positions (I only had to do so once in my long career, when I played a wounded rifleman in an awesomely dismal civil war saga and had to hide my inability to carry a tune), so, even as I invented the novelty, I abandoned it, retaining only the "push, push" chorus and the pregnant line, "The innocence in me heals me." This line I put in the mouth of an actor playing a former actor (who also can't sing), now an aging director/playwright, who was once an innocent young boy with golden locks (as I imagined him), but is these days lamenting the unhealed sadness of his life. His first movie was a smash hit, but everything after that bombed, as they say (and said) in the scandal sheets. Even his deep voice became a joke, mockingly imitated by the world's comedians. The industry in time came to shun him, and he was reduced finally to playing suburban theaters with idiotic audiences or to taking bit parts—bomb fragments—in stupid films, with even stupider commercials, desperately needed cash machines on the side. Until they didn't want him for that either. This was the painful rise-and-fall plot I had decided to develop.

All the young actresses teasingly called me "Dreamboat," which I have adopted now as the title of this work-in-progress. Thus, it's a reminiscence of sorts. It was never clear, even in the author's mind, how much Dreamboat's early fame was due to the quality of his performances, and how much to his being such a pretty boy, but, whatever the cause, all too quickly it turned sour. His gorgeous shock of golden hair darkened and fell out, leaving a bald pate with a waxy shine, bouts with sciatica cost him his posture, and over time he shriveled up like a raisin, becoming little more than a skeleton with a skull on top. A scythe was all he lacked for a *danse macabre*.

Which is what, sitting here tonight, alone in this cramped lightless theater, I was attempting to choreograph—a final *danse macabre*—when that wretched woman, wallowing in mock-innocence, crashed ruthlessly in on me, disrupting my creative train of thought. It's not easy to get that sluggish engine chugging along again, but the essence of my working script, as best I can reconstruct it, was the incorporation of a disturbingly comic parade of cavorting but ghastly skeletons into a brutally serious comedy about the terror of meaninglessness, and that's the concept I return to now. Sometimes I am overtaken by the desire to hasten the end of humanity on earth and close down the horror, but what spares it, beyond my own ineptitude, is that, in its tragicomic way, it's the only thing in the entire cosmos that's remotely interesting; on the other hand, once all those who might miss it are no longer around . . .

My original hope was to premiere *Dreamboat* in a charnelhouse, but I don't know if charnel-houses even still exist or what they look like if they do, it was the *word* I was seduced by. This stage, being to hand, must needs suffice. I plan to employ the usual accoutrements of blood-sucking bats, owls, ghostly wails, and black cats, along with the devil playing his fiddle all night long until the rooster crows, fiddling being an old knack that I can brush up on for my own supporting role in the show. No chance for costume changes, the green room is no bigger than a clothes closet, but hopefully it contains a ragbag of props and costume bits.

I've seen a senile ancient out there, hobbling mindlessly about on his stick, and I'm hoping to cast him as the aging playwright, a kind of clown's role, assuming that I can trick—or, if necessary, force—the old man into appearing on-stage from time to time. He already has the look of a sad-faced clown, and we can complete the semblance by costuming him in motley, with baggy britches and a polyurethane red nose, plus maybe a too-small straw boater on a chin strap. At the very least, we should get a few laughs out of the old buzzard, and he'll fit in well with the zombies.

I may have been talking out loud, a bad habit worsening with age, because some woman sitting behind me asks, "Do you think that's fair?" I recognize the voice as that of the irritating woman with the double chin. She has not exited, after all. If she has discovered this little refuge, others, alas, will surely follow. What in this whole sorry world is fair, I might sensibly have retorted, but pursuing the dialogue would be as meaningful as conversing with the void. No time for such frivolities. Your amiable conversationalist wishes only to complete his final opus and then to commune with his own demise, which I believe, if that disturbance I felt when the woman first came in here was its warning sign, is her cheery farewell gift to us.

I will need an assistant, someone to tame the personal elements, perhaps that friendly lad in the soft black jacket—but it may already be too late. The house lights flicker, come on throughout the auditorium, exposing its seediness. A group of partygoers floods in, apparently wishing to utilize the little theater for a wedding, according to the noises they make. They are led by a stolid woman of authority who would also seem to be the bride. I spoke earlier with an elderly mustachioed gentleman whom I assumed at the time to be her husband, but maybe they were only friends. He is not the groom-to-be, but that man is also familiar. Perhaps he owns or co-owns the penthouse.

My instinct tells me to make a hasty exit, but my ego demands that I stay; they are casting for the preacher, and, having played such a role on occasion, I find myself volunteering for the part. I've missed life on the stage, and perhaps others here will stay to perform in my midnight entertainment. Am I only providing a distraction from an inherent weakness? "Self-awareness can be fatal," that bearded gentleman warned me earlier, smiling his gap-toothed smile. His long-windedness is notorious. Like most amateurs, he lacks a proper sense of timing, goes on too long for fear of going on too briefly. I made a lame joke at the time about the condition being, fatal or not, fetal, which caused him to lift his fedora disdainfully and turn away.

But, yes, I seem to have been born to write for the theater, exploring society for plots and characters, but always dramas suffused with horror, for that's who I am, just as the bearded man saw. There is no help for the human animal, but we go on pretending there might be, writing our way through the hopelessness, our words leading us not to the light, but to eternal darkness. Which is what I've always loved about the theater, how it leads us always to the light, especially a theater as bright and cheerful as this one. It's the perfect setting for this marriage between two such lovely people—they're so *right* for each other!—in which I've been chosen by the bride herself to be one of her personal bridesmaids. I'm so lucky!

The bald man, who my girlfriend says was once a famous actor—his girl fans all called him "Dreamboat"—was already in the little theater when we got here. Apparently, he has agreed to serve as the officiant and help the couple tie the knot, so maybe he came here first and turned on the lights. My friend says he even has preacher credentials, which goes nicely with his enthusiasm for zombies, but as it's a second or third wedding for two older people, almost at the zombie stage themselves, it hardly matters. My girlfriend told me that the man took up writing when he didn't know what else to do, and became the author of many fabulous scripts for plays and films, now mostly seen on social media and the late-night reruns—ageless movie classics like *Voodoo Sex Party* and *A Dark Place* and the grisly *Forever After*, which is about being buried alive and is so scary that, after several viewings, I still haven't made it to the end.

I don't know why, but for some reason I feel close to the seedy old gentleman. It's as though we share, or have shared, something intimate, though I can't imagine what kind of intimacy that might be, except maybe that we both love horror movies. He may once have been good-looking, like older people claim, though that's hard to believe when you see him now. I feel toward him the way I might feel toward my father, if Dad hadn't got married so many times to so many different ladies. Why do people do that? It's so selfish and really hard on the kids, though at least Mom didn't stick us in an orphanage. Well, maybe the bald man has also married a few times, and I will, too, probably. The kids can and do make it somehow on their own.

Take my girlfriend, for example, who grew up in an orphanage, even though she had real parents. They had split and formed new families, so they decided to get rid of the old one, and found an orphanage that believed crossed eyes were good luck and would accept her. My friend said she really didn't care. The people at the orphanage were a bit rough at the edges maybe, but mostly more fun than her parents were, and my friend has turned out completely normal. Just goes to show. One of the nuns was even cross-eyed. The orphanage was nominally Catholic, and a priest would visit from time to time to give all the girls a hug and pat their little behinds. She said that naughty things sometimes happened in the orphanage, but at the time she didn't think of them as naughty, even when they hurt. She loved it there. Until her best friend was killed. Then the police came and the orphanage was closed. For a while, she was locked up in a juvenile prison, but she ran away by hiding in a clothes basket. That's what she says anyway. And I believe her, it's mainly how families work nowadays, though I hang on to hopes for something more like what happens in the movies. The way people *look* at each other, for example. I want somebody to look at *me* like that, and for longer than two minutes.

There are lots of fantastic people in this wedding party with whom I could imagine sharing an intimacy of the commoner sort, starting with the best man. He's so yummy! He even carries a walking stick with a pearl handle! My friend and I have had him in our sights all night, since way before the groom even proposed, if that's how it worked. "I could fall in love with him," I say, and my girlfriend, pushing her dark glasses up her nose, says, "I only want some healthy guy's dick. I don't care whose it is, only *that* it is and it works." She always has something funny to say.

All the girls are gushing over the best man, but, as my friend says, peering one-eyed up at me over her dark hornrims, none of them are as pretty as me, not even close. Smarter, sure, who isn't? But it takes a while to figure smarts out, and time just flies by at parties. Dummies can shine in places like this, especially if they're pretty girls like me, who are fun to be around. All I want is for everybody to find true happiness, with all my heart I do! And my girlfriend says, that counts for a lot in the dating game. I'm pinning my hopes on the best man, but he's not the only duck in the pond, there's a slew of groomsmen and ushers as well. The bride's a real humdinger of an organizer. I bet she's already figured out how to throw herself a bridal shower!

The best man is a bit older than me, he even has a distinguished streak of gray at his temples, but he's so gorgeous he *seems* younger, and anyway it's not like we'd be doing anything serious like getting married or having babies. At a party, you just try to be friends, and find a spot where you can be friends together, even if only for a few minutes. It doesn't matter if you're married or not, or even if you came to the party with someone else. So far, though, he hasn't even looked my way. Maybe when the ceremony begins, I can catch his eye. My girlfriend says he looks like a heartbreaker, but that's OK, I'm ready. "It's better than nothing," I tell her, "which is what a little boy who opened his short pants and showed me his little peewee once said." My friend laughs, pushes her sunglasses up her nose, and gives me a big hug.

The bride, who seems to be the boss of everything, comes striding down the aisle to announce that the wedding is about to begin, everyone should assume their proper places. Quite likely, she's the one who proposed. She is trailed by the groom with a drink in his hand, smiling sheepishly as though embarrassed by all the fuss being made. The bride is wearing a corsage she must have found somewhere. By the look of it, it might have been on a corpse. That's a scary thought, but the only thing that really scares me is getting trapped in a horror movie and not able to breathe. Of course, if reality is only a kind of horror movie, like my friend says, then we're all trapped, even if we can all still breathe.

The best man brushes right past me, stroking his handsome thin moustache. He's very intent on the ceremony at hand, no time for me, so I glance around at the other men and boys, picking out those who seem friendliest. It's hard to choose, they're all cute. That one wearing cashmere with bluejeans, for example, or the boy in the black leather jacket. The matron of honor is a very proper lady in a dazzling pearl-encrusted evening gown. Maybe she knew about the wedding and dressed for it, or maybe they chose her for how she was dressed. I'm a touch jealous, but only for a second, because the best man is staring at me over his shoulder. He winks solemnly, and my heart skips a beat.

A nun, who has come to bless the union, enters in a bright red tunic and a veil pinned to her jaunty coif. She doesn't smell very good, but she's pretty in a grim sort of way, and she makes serious what's mostly just a fun thing. She's a petite size and has a wicked little smile. If she weren't a nun, she'd probably be just one of the girls. She moves as though on rollerblades to where the loving couple are to set to seal their marriage with a kiss, hikes her crimson tunic, squats and—*pees on the floor!* Then she scuffs at the spot with her little black oxfords like a puppy, trying to scratch it away or else making it her own! *Wow!* I don't know *what* to think! The bride has a shocked sour look on her face, but the groom laughs and raises his glass naughtily to the nun. The bride takes her place above the nun's scuffed puddle, resolutely throws away her elaborate script, and the whole ceremony is over in five surly minutes.

Which is five minutes too long for me. The best man has been sneaking urgent glances at me all the time like in the romance

119

movies (he *loves* me!). "Honest," I say as soon as the wedding's over, "I wish I was your heart's desire! It would make me the happiest girl in the whole world!" The borrowed line by someone smarter than me seems to work. He takes my arm and leads me through the actors' little dressing room into a bedroom I didn't know was back here, locking the door behind us. He kisses me so hard I'm afraid my lips will bleed, and his hands are all over me! My heart is pounding like crazy! This must be love, I think, feeling an ecstatic tingle though my whole body. Or else, it's fear. He's so *fired up!* Maybe the nun's peeing in public got him over-excited.

"True love is like a light that can never be hidden!" is what I mean to say, but I only get as far as "true love" and the next thing I know we're both naked, my underthings ripped away. I know older men are less patient with preliminaries, but it's happening way too fast. Will it hurt, I wonder, and, as though to answer me, he shoves me face down on the bed and starts poking at my bottom. *"Wait a minute!"* I cry out, but he claps his hand over her mouth, shove my cock up her ass. She fights back, but it's too late, I'm in deep and hammering away, probably ruining her rubbery little rectum. She's tries to scream, so I put a chokehold on her, applying my walking stick to her windpipe. It's futile for her to resist, but I don't tell her that, her flailing about is part of the pleasure. No, it's the *essence* of it.

Fucking women while they're being throttled, as I found out while still a kid, is not only the best way of getting off, it's my *only* way. Without a lady's life being squeezed out beneath me, I'm limp as a rag. Mostly I buy dispensable prostitutes to exercise these basic human rights, but sometimes I find a hot underage slut like this one. They're more trouble, but, in their open-eyed shock and innocence (call it innocence), they're irresistible. I'd been watching her; she seemed to be on the make, pretty enough to arouse the gonads, dumb as a stump, and all alone up here except for a cheerful bespectacled twit about her age. Naturally, I want to let everybody live, I'm a decent fellow, do unto others, etc., but I rarely have a choice. In truth, I never do. If one of them survives, game over. So, instead, I let them live as long as possible under me. Living as long as you can is what it's all about, isn't it? I know that, when it's crunch time for me, I'll always ask for one more minute. And then another.

I can feel the pressure mounting in my groin—this is going to be *good!*—but hold off a few extra heartbeats, releasing my thumbs from her neck veins to allow her a wheezing facedown breath. Sometimes, in that stuporous moment before they die, their carotids closed off and their brains devoid of oxygen, they call me their savior, their god, but mostly they die cursing me. I'm OK with either, though I prefer—oh oh! *here it comes!* can't stop it!—*Omigod!* You're *terrific,* I whimper into her bloodless ear! *Ohhh FUCK!!* I—*ahhh!*—*LOVE* you! And for that moment, while my body is being drained, I *do,* I *really* do!

And then it's over. Ancient history. About five minutes of it at the outside. I douche away the blood and shit in the little john off the bedroom, take a bruised piss. There's a laundry chute in there, so I stuff her corpse down it. The body escapes my grip and drops precipitously. I grip the chute door and peek in. Looks bottomless. Of course, penthouses don't have basements, do they? What this one has instead is a kind of built-in garbage disposal unit. Interesting.

Time to put in an appearance. I tuck my shirt in, glance around for any telltale disturbances beyond the bloodied bed (I give the blankets a concealing toss), head out. The little theater where the wedding was staged has been abandoned, except for the bald man who officiated the travesty, nose down on the stage floor as if sniffing at the nun's urine, and a scrawny goateed guy in the dimly lit back row with a bouncing beribboned head in his lap. "This is better than what grandma did," he moans behind me, as I plant my walking stick under my arm and step out onto the crowded terrace.

I recognize many of the wedding party milling about out here on the roof and pause to chat with them, drifting from guest to guest, establishing my presence among them, my eye out the while for the little bridesmaid's cross-eyed friend. She hides her defect behind dark sunglasses with dark tortoise-shell frames, even at night, so she should be easy to spot. I'm ready for her with a canned response to any question the stupid girl might ask, or insinuation she might make. She is, however, nowhere to be seen. She probably supposed the bridesmaid had gone home, went there herself. Maybe. But: eyes open. Ignore the great wines being poured. Water only. Stay vigilant. Stay cool.

The principal topic out here is the bride's abrupt cancelation of the reception party. According to one of the groomsmen, a longhaired young man who looks decidedly out of step with the dress code, it would seem that, during the climactic smooch, the bride bit the groom's lip clean through. He left, cupping the bubbling blood in his hands, and the bride, still in a fury, canceled the reception. The groomsman also said that the bride started to throw her ring away, then, more frugally, pocketed it instead. What the guests seem to miss most, there being an abundance of food and drink supplied by the penthouse hosts, are the customary public confessions of the bride and bridegroom, and in particular the comically embarrassing tales of past loves and rumored current ones.

I say hello to the lady who was my counterpart as the matron of honor, a reserved woman, whose gown is decorated with pearls, which may or may not be real, and who speaks with a snobbish accent, which also may or may not be real. Channeling her classy style, I congratulate her on the elegance with which she performed her part in the ceremony. She acknowledges this fawning display with a shrug and a tolerant smile. She has a less elegant habit, I note, of chewing her fingernails. Her bent nose resembles that of a bird of prey as it pecks at her fingers. Conversations on the terrace are dominated by the nun's recent performance, but the owlish woman not only avoids the topic, she pretends not to have seen it, even though she was close enough to get peed on. I ask her about the bride's flash of lip-biting anger after the exchange of vows, and she has no opinion, other than to remark that men are not always on their best behavior and are too easily excused for their lapses. The amused look she gives me, suggests that, as I'm a man, I must therefore be no less guilty. I shrug and smile sheepishly, pleased at how I'm getting on.

Beyond the matron of honor, there's a section of the peripheral fence that has been violently bent away, the flower bed in front of it trampled. Hard to know what happened, though there's a heavily bearded man in a rumpled fedora staring thoughtfully at it as though he might be trying to figure things out. An amateur detective? I kiss the matron's chewed, bejeweled fingers and take my leave of her, walk over to introduce myself to him, not to learn anything from him, but to deflect any peculiar notions he might be entertaining.

At that moment, a portly young man in a bright plaid jacket and a pair of lady's pink panties wanders confusedly into the area, his testicles dangling darkly on either side of the twisted silk string in the middle, loses his balance, and finds himself sliding in the mud toward the precipice at the edge of the roof. His feet churn madly, trying to right himself—I start forward, but the bearded man is faster, grabbing the chubby lad's gaudy jacket and hauling him to safety. "All those poor people wanted," the man says, regarding the muddy incline, the crushed fence, "was to watch the moon rise." Fatboy does not even acknowledge his rescue with a "thank you," but wobbles away, bewildered, muttering to himself, hairy pot belly bulging over the waistband of the dirty silk underpants. "I feel, in the extremest sense of the word, a stranger here," the bearded man murmurs melancholically.

I remark briefly on the panty-clad fellow's rudeness, and then, getting only a professional grunt in reply, ask the man—whom some have called a philosopher and a wise man, others an inquisitive conman with a predilection for nubile young ladies—how it happens that we were the ones invited. "Do you think we just got caught in a net meant for bigger fish, or were we all, instinctively, obeying some compelling algorithm?" Rather than answer, the man, true to his nature maybe, but startling me nonetheless, asks about the pretty young thing and her strabismal friend, both last seen in my company. "I haven't a clue," I reply coldly. That's at least technically true. Time for that beer, after all.

At the family bar, there's a new bartender, a short blondish middle-aged man wearing a leather apron and a puffy chef's hat down around his large pink ears. His conversations are larded with lame jokes and dangling punchlines, but, in and around all the yeh-heh-hehhing, I gather that, when he went for another drink, he found nobody tending bar (I think I've seen the missing gentleman), so he poured his own, pouring for a few others when asked, and thus, one pour leading to another, becoming the de facto bartender, a role he clearly relishes. I say something about his doing a terrific job filling in for the regular guy, and he holds up his half-empty martini glass and declares: "I'm like the gentleman who wakes up in the morning with nothing to do and goes to bed with it only half done!" And he doubles up with wheezing laughter, tears in his eyes.

In the kitchen, on my way back to the terrace, I find the cook on his cane, now without his chef's hat, fuming against a gang of tough young women, some heavyset, others thin as kindling, one of the skinny ones covered in freckles, top to, I suppose, bottom. Did they steal his hat? They stick their tongues out at him, make rude noises. They seem to be trying to lure him out of the kitchen. To do what? They're just children, really. The clumsy old cripple shakes his cane at them, falls over, as they dance teasingly around him. He's mindless. Dangerous. Mad maybe. He struggles to his feet. I duck back out under the terrace lights. It's late. The sky's black behind the lights.

Someone is touching my elbow. A ghostly touch, and, were I of a mystical bent, I might read into it more than it deserved, but I know who it is and she's nobody's ghost. I turn to look into her crossed eyes, half-hidden by the dark sunglasses. "Yes?" I ask, but she has taken my hand and is already leading me toward the double doors. Nobody up here knows her. It's clear what she wants. I also want it. The matron of honor at the wedding, with whom I was talking just before she was abandoned by the disintegrating wedding party, is standing near the doors, with a stern, disapproving look on her hawkish face, but it's an expression that, alas, only quickens me. The laundry chute beckons. This time, I'll watch. In the interest of science, of course. Ah, what a shameless horror life is! The pretty boy passes close by us girls, visibly shuddering, stroking his thin moustache as though underlining a racy thought. His walking stick wags jauntily in his armpit like a brag. Or a threat, same thing. There's something weird about him, something not quite human, whatever that could be. It passes into me for a moment like a real thing, then it's gone. Did I just catch some of his weirdness? Oh wow! My imagination is inventing things. He's cute, but he's been cute for too long.

Cuter is the little girl providing arm candy for the zit-pitted fatface with the gold nose ring, who is said to own this luxe layout. You'd have to be pretty stupid to bed down with a roughhousing lardbelly like him, no matter what he's worth, but, by the look of her, showing off her lovely big bottom in a pleated skirt, stupidity is one requirement she can probably fill. "Ain't that the fuckin' berries?" the big fellow yawps, spewing a mouthful of deviled egg. Some of it lands on Arm Candy; she calmly brushes it away, unleashes a dimpled smile. Her trademark.

"Hey, wasn't that dude the barguy when we arrived?" asks one of my Thuguette sisters, punching my arm and pointing at a scrawny kid with a goatee and sideburns, clearly stoned out of his mind.

"Looks like him," I say, "except he's missing a couple of teeth." So is my sister. She probably thinks it's cute. The guy is pretty wasted, like he's given up on life itself. They're getting smashed on that bottle they're sharing, instead of breathing, all three having forgotten what it is to be young. Happens to everybody. The old middle-aged broad is already dead to the world, the other boyo in the ripped jeans and sweaty Stet is blotto, they're a sad lot, but you've gotta envy them. Mindlessness may be the only survival option left on this sick planet.

Buddies of the big boy have also shown up out here on the terrace, popping their knuckles, making raunchy comments about whoever walks past, whistling at them like you'd whis-tle at a dog. A bulky woman with humungous tits, subbing for the regular serving lady, whistles back at them. The men grab their trousered crotches and shake what's in there at her. She sets out a tray of mini lemon cheesecakes and pickle roll-ups, and then, with a shimmy of her own enormous butt, offers to take the whole gang of them on, one at a time or all together. They look away, sniggering sheepishly, and wolf down fist-fuls of pickles and cheesecakes. I snatch a small cheesecake while there's still one left. The substitute serving lady winks and laughs a horsey laugh, offers me another from her pants pocket. I hand it to a Thuguette sister and wink back. "Right on, kid!" the fat lady says.

She means well, but I'm not all that happy at being called "kid." It's a kind of putdown for girls my age, though it's probably better than being called "Freckles" or "Dotty"—as I speak, some evil asshole behind me is whistling for his dog "Spot"—and I have to admit I'm still feeling frisky as a kid, hot, ready for whatever. Except maybe another birthday. Fourteen's been a horror show, fifteen's bound to be worse. The only thing good about it is that it's when I stop being a "girl" and become a "young woman." Big deal.

Everything's going wrong with the world—it's not *up* shit creek, it *is* shit creek—and it may not last our lifetimes, pathetic fly-bys that they are. By the time I'm fifteen, I may be afloat on a planet gone adrift, scared to die, and suckered into all the survivalist crap, aching for the carefree time when I was fourteen; it happens to everybody else, doesn't it? Life, death, it's a one-way street, and fifteen is its no-parking zone.

Too much has to be dumped every year to make room in the brain for the new survival strategies, as Teach terms them. It's what we call "forgetting." Though why are we so taken with the idea of survival anyway? Some people want to hang on until eighty or ninety, but they're either too chicken to bugger off the sick planet voluntarily or else they're completely screwed up. If there's anything like a god-thing, it cares zip about people. I asked the bearded dude about it, and, echoing everybody else, he said: Don't give it up cheaply, life's all you have or will ever have. But if "all" is not enough? Come on, man. Get real! I have to say, I do feel comfortable around the old guy. He's like the grand-dad I never had, even if, like a lot of old guys, he can be pretty grumpy. I just learned the word "misanthrope." Fits him to a T.

Naturally, I've joined all the protest marches; in fact, I met the gang at one. At the time, they were marching against Death; not my favorite cause, smacks of the insanity of religion, but it touches on things I believe in, at least some of the time. In my more activist mode. The Thuguettes were there to protest suicide cults and climate change, and I could march for that, and bellyache at the same time about the inane prioritization of life, at least that of the human animal. It was fun to march along in the sunshine, arm in arm, chanting "Death to Death," even if we all meant something different by it. We became pals in the end, best pals really.

Night is deep into its lead balloon phase, with strings of diodes laced about overhead to beat back the creepy shadows. The grotesquely overweight server is still handing out goodies, the piss-ugly Cookie in the kitchen churning out bags of them as fast as she can get rid of them. We're going to have some fun with the crip, a hard man with a history of prison time for murder, when he comes wobbling out through the kitchen door, teased out by my Thuguette sisters. If the big serving lady doesn't get in the way: her eye is on the rich owner, the fat pig with the nose ring, and, trying to snag his attention, she keeps moving around, getting her big bod in the way of anything moving. Chasing the owner puts her on a collision course with Arm Candy, who may be looking sweetly the other way, but clearly knows what's going down. More comedy in the offing, with the smart money on the big lady with the muscular boobs. It's not clear what's doing with the former server. Off chasing a singing career maybe. She sure knew how to unloose a ditty, and she was well past the point of no-return, so why not? No future for old ladies up here.

Or maybe she got the same endgame treatment as Teach. Teach was a great guy who treated everyone—even me—like a grown-up. At his age, most people have forgotten what it is to be young, but not Teach. We followed him up here to protect him, and we fucked up. He's why Cookie has made the top of our shit list, a bad man who deserves whatever pain we can dish—*Hey! Look out, here he comes!* The kitchen door bangs open and, like a gimpy old hog, Cookie stumbles forth on his cane, thin black cigarillo between his teeth. His butt is being switched by my sisters, but he doesn't seem to feel it. Maybe everything's dead down there. The rest of us are waiting for him. We surround him and, wary of his killer hands, crowd him toward the greasy carpet of the trampled garden. Doesn't take long. He loses his footing and soon enough, all he can think about, clawing away at the mud beneath him, is getting his balance back. He grabs two of my sisters, one by a wrist, the other by the ankle, dragging them down with him, but we tickle him mercilessly with long prods, and he lets them go. Everybody's laughing, this is the grown-up world, lots of fun on the slippery slopes. Show-offs, excited by the comedy, throw themselves onto the mud and imitate his crippled clawing, though when Cookie, in tears, poor guy, slips over the edge, groaning "I am . . . sad . . . ugly . . . man," the fun seems to go out of the game. The comedian who follows him over the edge is quickly forgotten, but Cookie is remembered, at least for the moment. Which is something like forever.

We check our watches. Action time: enter the theater and secure a section in the audience from which to heckle the actors. Liberate the girls, drive the boys crazy. Or vice versa. It's a small theater, so there won't be a lot of empty seats, but we can clear a few; there are warriors among us who relish pasting any sucker who dares to object. On the way in, I glimpse the cross-eyed chum of the bridesmaid, all alone, and, with a thumb-jerk, invite her to join us. She grins and shakes her head, but blows a kiss. She looks mussed up. Where has she been? There's an unhappy old lady guarding the double doors, but we push past me, deplorable young women that they are. They tend to be on the meaty side or else frightfully skinny, a gang of homely ill-behaved teenagers, or recent teenagers, whose goal in life seems to be the discomfiting of everybody else. They take pride in being bullies, calling themselves "girl-thugs," or something like that. These are not people I want to know.

It began so differently! I was gratified to be chosen to be the Matron of Honor for a bride I hadn't met before. If the marriage was a bit unusual (the bride had been widowed earlier that same day), one could only be reassured by the lavish penthouse setting, the elegant ceremonial stage, seemingly built just for the wedding, the multitude and wealth of the guests. But all that changed with the bizarre behavior of a malodorous nun, ostensibly come to bless the marriage and add an aura of piety to the festivities, and nothing has been quite the same since. The rage of the mortified bride, having had her much-ballyhooed marriage ceremony rained upon, so to speak, by a wayward sister of the cloth, is entirely justified. I would have felt the same. Even the groom, men being men, was somehow compromised, and suffered her righteous displeasure. What was amazing was that she went ahead with the ceremony at all, even in its abbreviated form.

She has recovered her aplomb, I should say, and is busy once more attempting to win others to her cause, if it is a cause and not mere self-aggrandizement. At the moment, she's presenting her case to a young man in a handsome soft leather jacket. As she confided to me earlier: "Once our procedures become familiar, ordinary people will more readily accept them as normal. Frequent usage makes a commonplace out of the uncommon." The power game, she plays it well.

When the young man leaves to reenter the theater, I approach her to thank her for the gift of being invited to serve as Matron of Honor at her splendid wedding. She winces, for it turns out that she has not merely obtained a legal separation from her new husband in the hours since then, she has, for the second time today, been widowed. An explanation for her tears, though probably not the cause. All this is happening too fast for me. I compliment her yet again on her good fortune and bid her adieu, determined to vacate the premises as soon as possible, not to embarrass myself further.

As I turn away, I am struck by an uncooked eggy thing. I don't know for certain who threw it, but the air is suddenly full of flying appetizers. A party game? I duck behind the substitute serving lady's broad back, the safest place to be out here on the roof, to wipe the egg yolk out of my eyes, worried about what may have splattered onto my dress. It was very expensive and bought on a whim especially for this party, which was supposed to be fancier than it really is. Though it's quite likely that the new serving lady was the person who launched the food fight with her own appetizers, she takes good care of me, deftly slapping away the flung appetizers, raw or cooked, and hurling her own, pitching them overhand like hardballs. I'm glad to have her on my side. There's apparently an endless supply of ammunition, for when the new oven is emptied, it simply refills itself! The sort of oven we all need! I'll have to ask how much they cost, but probably only rich people like the penthouse owner can afford one.

When there's a brief let-up in the free-for-all, I ask the caterer's left ear what happened to the other caterer, the woman with the singing voice, and she explains, while batting away hors d'oevres, that she was an unrepentant criminal who was executed for her crimes by being tossed off the terrace. "You shoulda seen the fat thing," she says, "kicking frantically at the nothing she was lying in, shitting her bloomers, and belting out gospel songs all the way down!" So, the caterer, too. Why do I worry that the list doesn't end there? Is it legal, I wonder, to execute prisoners so quickly? And by such means? Well, perhaps. I don't know a lot about the law. The server spies an elderly lady, fleeing desperately on a walker, and nails her with a cheesy tater tot.

"The sad thing tried to fly away," the serving lady adds cheerfully about her predecessor, or maybe about the old lady on the walker, "but her wings let her down."

As the food fight rages on, the loudspeakers announce a tribute concert tonight for the deceased composer, featuring his last great, but unfinished work. His violent death was a scandal; now, it is widely accepted, even celebrated. How quickly we get used to anything! A blind former student of the old serialist has fashioned a less austere version of his final work, which the composer himself said was impossibly difficult ("It needs to be read, not played!") and was still in-progress. There are those who dispute this interpretation of the old composer's remarks, arguing that his transparency is of another sort, requiring a different linguistic form for its expression, and that his compositions were *always* "in-progress": it was a working principle of sorts. But the blind ex-student insists that his own twelve-tone score is more expressive of the lifework of the old composer, whom he describes as the true champion and preserver—a fact carefully hidden in his more innovative work—of music's grand tradition. This is the view that prevails. Normally, I'd stay long enough to hear the concert and judge for myself, but I must leave immediately.

The new piece will no doubt prove to be more controversial than the composer's own violent death, setting off a flood of scholarly papers on the fulfillment—or betrayal—of the man's original intentions and last wishes. In its revised version, it is

scheduled to be performed as a prelude to tonight's theater pro-
duction of *Dreamboat*, with its dance of the skeletons. A well-
known playwright, an eccentric fellow with a shiny pate and
whiskery chin, is directing what he ballyhoos as "a paean to
meaninglessness." Many of the party guests have been offered
a role in the entertainment, myself included—a role politely
refused, of course, on grounds that I don't plan to stay that late.
I glance at my watch: good grief, it's nearly midnight! I have lin-
gered too long! There have been problems with the house elevator. Does the theater have its own, I wonder?

The food fight flares up briefly, targeting now a senile old
man, who has staggered (was he pushed?) out of the theater
doors onto the terrace, lost and confused. He wears a clownish costume of a plastic red nose, a funny little straw hat, tied
under his chin, and baggy piebald pants with holes in both
knees. They pummel him with steamed clams, potato skins and
frosted bananas, he grinning unflinchingly through the barrage.
The playwright-director hurries out to rescue him, just as the
overweight owner with the nose ring sticks out a foot and trips
up both the old man and the director, laughing a loud *hrooff-haff*
laugh, as though he's just done something wonderfully entertaining. It find it more sad than funny, but then, I don't laugh
at most jokes either. The substitute caterer delivers the coup de
grace with a grape jelly meatball, aimed at the back of the old
fellow's head. The director, sitting up, instructs his assistant, a
docile young man in a black chamois jacket, to port the clown

back into the theater, and he does so, picking him up like a pile of broken sticks and carting him off through the double doors.

The penthouse owner and the young gold-digger on his arm attempt to follow them in, but the serving lady puts her blue-jeaned mass in their way. She cozies up to the big man, fondling him through his stretch dress pants; he grins obsequiously around his half-chewed cigar. The young lady at his side kneels to change her shoes to golfer's cleats, walks over to the slippery slope to test them, then shouts out—"HEY, FATSO!" She sticks her thumbs in her ears and wags her hands like donkey ears. The serving lady takes the bait. She galumphs toward her, a wicked grin on her determined face, soon loses her footing, and, cursing everybody, legs churning, disappears off the edge. The pretty lady in the pleated skirt takes the owner's arm and leads him away; he follows hesitantly, but looks askance at her, somewhat stricken.

I am myself somewhat stricken. It all happened so fast! This was not an execution, there was nothing legal about it, it was *murder!* And taken for granted by all those standing around! These are not my people! This crowd is mostly a hard lot, who are convinced they are the "good people," and the more wrong-headed they are, the more they believe that. In the past, I would have denounced them all as willfully ignorant, but as the old bearded philosopher warned me, "To define problems, seek solutions, is to live the tragic life." Alas, rarely able to desist, such a life would seem to be my fate. But not now, not yet . . .

Before returning to the theater, the director pauses for a quick smoke, and, in his blind haste, lights two cigarettes at once. He seems mystified by the choice they present him, staring at them through his cracked spectacles. He lights a third, then—after an *aha!* moment—throws one of them away and tucks the other two into opposite corners of his mouth, drawing on both of them at the same time. "I meant it as a comedy," he declares in a *sotto-voce* mutter, while releasing two separate plumes of smoke, the very image of indecision. I want to ask him about the possible existence of a theater elevator, but I'm not sure he even sees me standing before him. He explodes with a roar—"BUT IT'S NOT FUNNY ANYMORE!"—sending his cigarettes flying and me staggering backwards. Then, he does look at me. "Hello, my dear," he says softly, a gentle smile above his jutting chin. "Are you here to try out for a part in my *danse macabre*?"

"*No!*" I yelp. I have to get *out* of here! "I'm not an actor! I'm only looking for the way—!"

"Everyone is an actor, dear lady. Don't worry, there are no lines to learn. You're now a part of our little drama. We're rehearsing as I speak. Come along now; perhaps you alone can save the day!"

And he seizes my arm in an iron grip, pulling me through the double doors into the darkness of the little lobby—"But I don't *want* to!" I cry—and on into the auditorium beyond.

It's a small theater, quickly filling up. Those unruly girls have taken up all the seats in the middle, everybody else paced in at the back or standing in the aisles. No matter, I don't need a seat, only freedom from this crazy man's bony hold on me and a safe exit. Everybody seems to know him and they back away as we charge through. I appeal to them for help, and get only laughter in reply.

The pregnant lady who was sprawled, knees high, on the carpet in the main reception room has been brought here as a kind of theatrical prop, and lies, still wailing, at one side of the stage. She draws large gaping crowds, adding to the general terror. Is she really pregnant or only showboating?

The bearded gentleman in the ratty fedora is sitting in the front row of the packed auditorium; he must have arrived early to get such a good seat. He's having an earnest word with one of those little troublemakers, a homely girl covered in freckles, proudly wearing her hideous spots like merit badges. Perhaps he's lecturing her on her misbehavior. His face expresses a wistfulness that we share, reminding me that, where earnestness is, there, also, is melancholy, or so I remark to myself as I gaze upon the sad freckled face of the little Thuguette. She's different from the other young women in her gang: she *thinks*. And, therefore, she *suffers*. She's a child of course, and has childish thoughts, but she understands reality in a way that the matron of honor cannot. Though she's very young, in her late-twenties at most, she's already fully aware of the joke she is in—it is the joke of life itself, cosmic and indecent—and she laughs aloud at its punchline. But she cries, too. Her spiritual beauty has me, if perhaps inappropriately, enthralled.

When she muscled in beside me ("I need to talk to my Dad," she said to the fellow in the polka-dot bowtie who was sitting there, lifting him right out of the seat and twisting his arm behind his back so hard he yelped), she wanted to know what I thought about love and loneliness. I was flattered that she recognized me as someone she could ask. I replied that loneliness was endemic to all mankind, and that people simply had to learn to live with it.

"I know that already, tell me something new. Tell me about love."

"Sure. People need to share their loneliness somehow with others. Love is what they call that sharing."

"You mean, if you love someone absolutely, it doesn't always make you feel less lonely?"

"I mean that loneliness is permanent and inescapable, while love is a flighty thing. It happens, or it doesn't, and the loneliness remains the same, regardless. Love won't get you out of it." There's an argument to be made that love is nothing more than the blind pull of an event like this penthouse party, but I knew it was not a notion she'd be happy with.

"That's not good news, but if you're trying to say that loneliness is stronger than love, I don't buy it. It's like that old story about the wind and the sun—one stiffens backbone, the other melts it, but they both figure. I think you're confusing loneliness with longing and love with sex." All too true, sad to say. "To tell it like it really is, though," she added, her expression softening then from admonishment to melancholy, "love's not much help either. It's just that *saying* so makes me feel less lonely." "You often feel that way?"

"All the time. When I was young, I saw a little boy catching grasshoppers and tearing their wings off. I was little, too, of course, it was a long time ago. When I asked him why he was doing that, he said he wanted to help them stop flying and start walking like people do, so they could all be friends. But the sad thing, the boy said, is that grasshoppers without wings just tip over and die." She paused a moment to mourn the dead grasshoppers. "Which is how life is. When you're fifteen, the wings come off, and you tip over into umpteen dead years of emptiness and loneliness. Not sure I want that."

"Ah, I see . . . Then how . . . If you don't mind my asking, how old are you now?"

"Promise not to laugh, OK? But lots older than you think. I'm already nearly fifteen, trying really hard not to be scared."

So, she's a child still, bright and feisty, but young enough to be my granddaughter. Not much chance I'd laugh. Cry, maybe. Love feeds off humankind like a deadly parasite. If I believed in aliens, I'd call it one. But when there's transgenerational accord, what's a mere difference in age?

Alas, granddad, nearly everything . . .

"I just saw something really crummy," my freckled interlocutor whispers now. "A man, who wasn't even crying, walked right to the edge, and stepped off."

I know who she's talking about, I saw him, too. I explain to her that, yes, there are those who prefer suicide in daylight to involuntary death in the dark. "I can empathize with the suicidal types," I add, conscious that I'm speaking to one, "but I can't do what they do. Instead, I've decided to live forever." I pause to clear my throat. "Until forever, whatever it is, stops." She laughs as I'd hoped she might, and I smile down at her, aware too late that I'm showing the clownish gap in my large front teeth. But what does it matter? If I'm right, *nothing* matters. The lights dim momentarily like a grim foreshadowing of what lies ahead. Do I tell her that forever may stop tonight? Do I tell *myself* that?

She and her friends came up here looking for their teacher, thinking he might be in trouble (maybe he is; they haven't found him yet), and she says she felt something jump into her when a member of the wedding party passed by. "I didn't like it. It felt like having a fidgety ghost up my ass, and the feeling didn't go away until we shoved past that mean old lady up there, who was doing her master-sergeant skit at the time out by the theater doors."

That lady's not so old, I want to say, but don't. I know what she's talking about, though. While the matron of honor was being dragged down the aisle to the stage, she was radiating a full-blown hysteria, which felt to me, second-hand, like the onset of a head cold, like catching a virus, and I sneezed. The woman was trying to adjust to the reality of an expanding world, but sometimes adjustment is just too hard. The tiny dressing room behind the stage suddenly became visible, the bedroom beyond, even the bathroom past that and the square door inside by the lavatory that leads to a cupboard or maybe to a laundry chute, all laid out like the plot of a story. The little Thuguette called it "weird." She's right, it *is* weird. But it's also real. Like the penthouse is real, the nun, the unavoidable and irreversible ending. Hysteria is not adjustment.

These thoughts are interrupted by the playwright bringing on-stage an old man dressed in the bloated piebald pantaloons of a clown. Reaching into the pants through a big hole at the knee, the playwright, wagging his long tufted chin, lifts one bony leg and puts it down, then the other one, up and down, both legs wrapped in red flannel. The orchestra plays echoey musical analogues. "Look! He's teaching the old guy how to dance!" laughs the little Thuguette at my side. The playwright steps back, smiling expectantly under his shiny dome. There's a slow drum roll, heightening expectations. The old man, muttering gloomily to himself, reluctantly lifts one leg, holds it, thinking hard, sets it down—then he abruptly drops his baggy pantaloons, tears off the red nose, and, in his ragged long johns, rear flap unbuttoned, limps petulantly away on his cane.

"Oh, no! I *knew* he was going to do that!" exclaims my companion, happy as a child at the circus.

The playwright starts to follow the old man, thinks better of it, dons the clown pants and nose, as well as a jacket, a couple of sizes too small, huge slapshoes, a bowtie with a blinking green light at the knot, oversized gloves, and a tiny straw boater on a chinstrap. The Thuguette claps enthusiastically and jabs me in the side with her elbow. The playwright, squinting through his cracked bifocals, slap dances, knees high, to the disorderly racket of the musicians. Who are now wearing skeleton costumes. If they *are* costumes.

The announced concert begins—or has begun. It is loud and cacophonic, or maybe they're only tuning their instruments. The auditorium and stage have stretched out to accommodate the musicians and the rapid gathering of party guests, crowding cheerfully into the aisles. Have they been brought to the theater, or is the theater being brought to them, the outside in effect moving inside? How else did they get the grand piano up there on the stage?

The nun appears, her silver cross glinting, undulating sedately to the unruly music, ostensibly that of the old serialist. She removes her veil, tossing it solemnly to an ancient Lothario, standing at the lip of the stage. "Go, girl!" he shouts in his rumbly voice. She is aging visibly. Her teeth are more prominent, and there are gaps in her grin. The Thuguette at my side gleefully wonders what's going on, what does it *mean*? Will she throw candy to the crowd?

There are small artificial trees, strung with colored lights. They cast a light less bright than yuletide tree-lights, so it's increasingly difficult to distinguish between the musicians and their audience. The edges of things are disappearing, or else my eyesight is worsening. The matron of honor is on-stage as well, now wearing only her bloomers, her large soft breasts freed from their brassiere, her sagging belly from its girdle. The old boy whistles at her. She clearly doesn't know what's happening, only knows she doesn't like it. The musicians bounce as they play, perhaps in imitation of her belly wobble. The pianist, a scrawny young man with oily dreadlocks, bobs about on the bench in front of the grand piano, hammering away furiously. That muddy patch: is it the slippery slope?

"What do you think about the piano guy?" the Thuguette asks. "He's very avant-garde, isn't he?" "He makes a lot of noise."

"Is that all you have to say? God! You're such a hopeless dweeb!"

I grunt in reply. The dweeb has to craft a proposition that confronts the altered reality and at the same time offers something meaningful to the child—complete freedom to live her own life on my money as long as it lasts, in exchange for her company and lots of conversation, something like that. She should probably move in with me. Granddad has to get another bed, of course.

While I'm thinking of her sleeping soundly in her little bed, and at the same time mulling over usable phrases, the grand piano and its bench start to slither down the muddy slope toward the edge! Before I can snatch at her, the Thuguette declares: "Well, I know a genius when I hear one," and she runs off to plant herself next to the pianist on his sliding bench!

I jump to my feet to rescue her from herself, but the way is blocked by the undulating nun, and I say something idiotic like, "Please! Let me by! I don't even belong to your damned religion!"

The piano is picking up speed, the pianist hammering away as though frantically trying to put the brakes on. The Thuguette joins him in his frenzied noise-making by striking the keys with her elbows. I push at the nun—there's the pop and crackle of shattering crystal and porcelain—but she still won't get out of my way! She reaches inside her tunic and offers me her breasts, which shrivel at my touch and quickly—too quickly—commence to rot.

I collapse into my seat with my hands full of indescribable gunk, just as the Thuguette and the pianist disappear over the edge. There is a crash and the pinging of piano wires, the ever more distant scrape of wood against stone. She is gone. I sit, too stunned to move. How does one, in this strange cruel life, avoid a hardening heart, a softening brain?

The nun, who has been punctuating the night with her parade of irregularities, now slowly strips off the rest of her habit, the coif and wimple and their black crape decorations, the scapular and detachable sleeves, the many aprons. All these things she flings to the audience around her, one garment at a time (an apron swats me in the face like a castigation), swaying ritually the while, the removal of each item a sacred act. The old roué crawls up onto the stage on his knobby knees. People are laughing, but I can no longer laugh with them. I have often said that I don't know what's coming, but be it what it will, I'll go to it laughing; I'm trying, but no laughter emerges. Not even a sardonic snort.

The nun embodies a dark amoral force at play up here, one that has no voice of its own, no desires, no purpose, no capacity to reason. Life and death mean nothing to this force. It carries on outside the self, but is experienced within. When people speak of a nameless dread, this is what they are usually talking about. I know; it has been tunneling through me all my life. Now, in particular. Despair, emptiness, aimlessness, they're all part of it, but they are not the thing itself, which exists apart from all thoughts about it. Add that it's universal and collective, and I feel like I've just been describing "love."

When it's time to remove her serge tunic, the nun pauses until she has everyone's close attention—then she grabs the pleated neck and, ripping it open, hauls the tunic over her head, exposing a wrinkled body and layers of underskirts, the hair on her head by now thin, white, and snarly. "Whoa!" exclaims the old profligate, backing hurriedly off the stage on his hands and knees. I peer into the shadows where the breasts were, trying to see something where nothing is. The ancient, crawling backwards, falls off the stage, audibly cracking his leg bone.

The underskirts are cast off slowly, one by one, until the nun arrives at her lacy old-fashioned drawers. The drawers are held up by a drawstring at the waist. With a sly look at the fallen old boy, she tugs on the knot, and, just as the drawers drop, she reaches for a zipper at her throat, unzips her body, and steps out of it. Her bones rattle in a kind of applause. The nun peels the thin rubbery flesh off her hands, finger by finger, like removing gloves. She takes off her face, puts the stiff white cornette back on her grinning skull, and reaches inside the woman on the floor. A bespectacled lady rises from the audience, announcing that she's a licensed midwife, and, together, they extract a tiny soft skeleton, which the nun presses to her ribs. The nun shows the lady where, within her double chins, her zipper is located, then steps in front of the musicians to lead them in an eerily festive high-kicking dance of the dead, joined by the infant skeleton's now-bony mother, wearing her pudendum between her dancing legs like a flower.

I have long believed that flesh is nothing but a costume for the terrified beast within, but I never imagined pulling it off like a jumper, which is how the nun, the lady, and the cavorting musicians free themselves of their bodies. They play a discordant triple-meter jig, their clicking bones marking the jaunty rhythm. Those in the audience who wish to join the dance are welcomed and shown where their zippers are. All goes smoothly, except when the zipper gets stuck, which can be severely painful, to judge by the frenetic rattling of bones. Some discard their flesh as though weary of it, others, planning to wear it again later, fold it up and lay it carefully to one side.

Those who turn down the invitation to the dance are unceremoniously thrown from the penthouse terrace by a skeleton in a cowboy hat. Some, like the ecstatic saxophone honker, bleating away, are too distracted by their holy madness, as the old evangelist would have it, even to find their zipper, but up here everything's a capital crime, even distraction.

When it's the turn of the bossy business woman, the one who played the chesty bride at the staged wedding, she heroically demands that they immediately cease and desist, else they'll be hit with a huge lawsuit. They simply, she cursing them tearfully, heave the officious lady off the roof. They don't laugh or cheer, it's all very businesslike. Her tossing leads to a rush from others to unzip and join the dancing skeletons, which seem to stay alive in their fleshless state, at least for a little while. The lady's number two, the contrabassist, has already joined the musicians and is now, anonymously, a loose string of clattering bones, his instrument confiscated and danced upon. The old serialist's score is not exactly dance music, but the skeletons are dancing to it.

The little tree-lights have been dimming steadily. They will soon go out. I wish I could find a more cheerful way to end my life, but the terror of meaninglessness and the death of the little Thuguette have somewhat undone me. I'm not thinking well; perhaps thought itself is a criminal aberration, worthy of erasure. But, though I am drawn to the idea of locating my zipper and joining the bony dance, I am fearful of losing my hard-earned consciousness. I don't know what I'll do.

ROBERT COOVER is the author of twenty-some books of fiction and plays, including *The Cat in the Hat for President* and *The Enchanted Prince*. He has been nominated for the National Book Award and awarded numerous prizes and fellowships, including the William Faulkner Award, the Rea Lifetime Achievement Award for the Short Story, and a Lannan Foundation Literary Fellowship. His plays have been produced in New York, Los Angeles, Paris, London, and elsewhere. From 1981 to 2012, he taught creative writing at Brown University, where he is T.B. Stowell Professor Emeritus in Literary Arts.